HEEL
TURN

HEEL
TURN

A Sam Quinton Mystery

KEVIN R. DOYLE

**CAVEL
PRESS**

Kenmore, WA

CAMEL
PRESS

A Camel Press book published by Epicenter Press

Epicenter Press
6524 NE 181st St.
Suite 2
Kenmore, WA 98028

For more information go to:
www.Camelpress.com
www.Coffeetownpress.com
www.Epicenterpress.com
www.kevindoylefiction.com

Cover design by Scott Book
Design by Melissa Vail Coffman

Heel Turn
Copyright © 2021 by Kevin R. Doyle

ISBN: 978-1-60381-295-5 (Trade Paper)
ISBN: 978-1-60381-296-2 (eBook)

Printed in the United States of America

To Marvel A. and Mike L., former bosses,
who provided me a livelihood while I got my act together.

CHAPTER ONE

IN THE MIDDLE OF A WEDNESDAY MORNING in September, with the droves of college students having recently completed their trek back to the city, Bernie Lyman sauntered into The Blaster, the gym I've owned for the last handful of years. I was over in the free weight section, no machines for The Blond Bomber, which was my name when I was a professional wrestler. I was trying, and failing, to do as many squats, with as much weight, as I used to do during my younger days. A softer man than me would have eased off as soon as his face started turning red.

Bernie entering the gym saved me from that sort of humiliation.

Even if I hadn't noticed him right off Bernard Lyman, Esq, always saunters into places. He never walks like a normal person, instead carrying himself with all the pomp and circumstance of a born winner in life. Considering his reputation, that pretty much makes sense.

However, if you only knew him by sight, you'd shake your head at his delusion.

Bernie is a fairly short guy, a little under five seven, and weighs about as much as an underdeveloped teenager. More than that, he looks like his most recent residence is a cardboard box under I-70. His hair always reminds me of the doctor in *Back to the Future*, though not as well styled, and most people living under overpasses would cringe at wearing the shabby clothes he does. Add in teeth stained a faint brown from years of heavy smoking, and you couldn't conceive the guy being successful at anything in life.

Then again, you know what they say about judging books and covers.

Bernie stopped right inside the door and glanced around. He took in the smattering of clients currently working their way to physical perfection, most of them housewives in their thirties and forties taking part in a spin class, before looking over my way.

Bernie, the most observant person I've ever met, never misses anything, and I was pretty sure he'd spotted me as soon as he entered but wanted a few seconds to ogle my clients.

However, he didn't make a big production out of it, and in only a few seconds continued in my direction, an odd expression on his face. Kind of a cross between his usual small smirk and a troubled frown.

"Ain't you getting a bit old for that, Blondie?" he asked as he came within a few feet of the squat rack.

I gritted my teeth and did five more reps, just to show him, before struggling the weight back onto the rack. I had a small sweat towel lying a few feet off to the side but figured that if Bernie saw me use it he'd think I was a sissy.

Or maybe I simply didn't want to admit to advancing age.

"Not yet," I said, hoping I wasn't grimacing at the burn in my thighs, "maybe someday."

Bernie, without a doubt the best criminal attorney in mid-Missouri (he'd gladly claim the entire state, including Kansas City and St. Louis), nodded. His face gave way to total frown.

"What's up?" I asked.

"Got a job for you, Blondie. If you want it."

Lots of people call me Blondie, hearkening back to my days in the professional wrestling ring when I went by the moniker of The Blond Bomber. And while I don't tolerate it from most, Bernie Lyman has been my lawyer for quite a while, gotten me out of more than one legal scrape, and usually only charges about a third of his actual rate, so I figured I could let the name slide. However, in all the time of our association, this was the first time he'd come to me instead of the other way around.

I glanced around the gym. Lisa Nolan, my young manager, was

leading the spin class, her bright red ponytail jiggering and jittering all over the place. Keri Eckland, a college sophomore Lisa had recently hired on a part-time basis, was going over the machines, making sure everything looked clean and spotless for the lunchtime rush.

One or two guys, including a regular named Harold Hammer who, no matter how much work he puts in, never seems to gain an ounce of muscle, were hard at it on the machines, grunting and straining their way to exhaustion.

All in all, things looked fairly good for one of my businesses. Stood to reason, though, that Bernie was here to talk about the other one.

"Let's go to the office," I said as I snatched up the sweat towel and dabbed my forehead.

Yep, he gave me a look as if I was a sissy.

We made our way back to my sparse, no frills office. I plunked myself behind my desk, and Bernie took one of the client chairs ranged in front of it. I leaned back, my legs feeling it by then. I don't quite get it. At two twenty-five I'm the same weight I was years ago, more or less. Therefore, I should be in the same shape, or at least that was my logical way of looking at it.

But I couldn't remember the quads burning as much in the past.

"What's the word?" I asked Bernie. I watched him squirming in his seat. Whatever was going on, it definitely had him excited.

"As of right now, I'm at least nominally your client, okay? Even if you end up turning down the work. Okay?"

Private investigator confidentiality isn't all they make it out to be on TV, though it can at least cover the bases. Far as that went, if the authorities ever did make some kind of stink, Bernie was my personal lawyer, so we could always fall back on that.

"A new client," Bernie continued. "Called the office just this morning. Not," he glanced at his knockoff Rolex, "an hour ago."

"Bernie," I said, "you're going to fidget yourself right out of that chair unless you get to it. What's this new client charged with?"

"Nothing," Bernie said, a wide smile splitting his face almost in two, "yet."

I peered closer at him.

"Let me get this straight. Are you hoping they'll be charged with something?"

"Not hoping, buddy. I know for sure. And when the charge comes, it's going to be a doozy."

I'd known Bernie for several years, and at the moment I couldn't remember him ever being that excited. I'd call him giddy, but I detected that underlying grimness in his manner, as if the seriousness of the situation was fighting with his natural tendencies.

I assumed he wanted me to play along, and I figured what the hell and went with it.

"Who's the client, Bernie?" I asked.

Although he could not possibly have grinned any wider, he did his best.

"Sheila Hampton," he said, his eyes damned near sparking.

Oh boy, I thought. That explained it.

Bernie Lyman, Esq, had nabbed himself one hell of a client.

CHAPTER TWO

SHEILA HAMPTON WAS ABOUT THE BIGGEST NEWS that had hit the state of Missouri in who knew how long. This despite the fact that for most of her forty-eight years she'd lived a fairly anonymous life. About a quarter century ago, at the time of her trial, she enjoyed momentary infamy. Didn't last though. After the sentencing and being shuttled off to prison for life, most of the community, not to mention the larger world, had pretty much forgotten about her. Until last week, when she suddenly became front page news around the country, putting Providence and Carson County on the map for all the wrong reasons.

She'd started life as Sheila Clark and had married Derek Hampton shortly before her twentieth birthday. At the time of their marriage, Derek was ten years older than Sheila. Kind of extreme, though not all that unusual considering that she was an absolute knockout and he was worth somewhere north of a hundred million dollars.

Derek Hampton had earned his money, as they say, the old-fashioned way. By inheriting it. His grandfather had been an early investor in AT&T, then taken the proceeds and diversified the hell out of the family interests. The old man's son, Derek's father, had managed the family money well, to the effect that by the time he died unexpectedly in a boating accident hardly anyone knew just how much money the family had or everything they owned.

There was some controversy at the time of the old man's death.

Derek was the youngest of three siblings, yet somehow he managed to vault over the other two to became chairman of the board of the family company. At the time, some financial folks around Providence expected there to be some sort of contention to the old man's will, but it never came about.

So no, it didn't seem that unusual that Sheila, who'd started her working life as a waitress in a local bar, had managed to snag a rich husband. Most people who knew the two probably considered the young Mrs. Hampton a typical gold digger who Derek would eventually cast aside for a newer model.

And who knows, maybe he would have. Except that he never had the chance. A couple of days after their third anniversary, shortly after midnight, Sheila made a frantic call to 911, screaming that someone had broken into their house and shot her husband.

The first wave of cops made it to the house within five minutes, but they were delayed by the fact that they couldn't get past the security gates at the front of the Hampton home.

"I DON'T GET IT, BERNIE," I said. "When did you start doing civil work?"

"Civil?" Lyman's eyebrows went up so far enough that I thought they'd disappear in the mangled nest that was his hair.

"Hampton's going to sue the state, right? False imprisonment?"

Bernie stared at me for a moment, then shook his head as if I was the slowest kid in class.

"I'm guessing you haven't caught the news this morning, huh?"

FROM ALL ACCOUNTS, WHEN THE POLICE made their way onto the grounds and in the house, they found one very dead Derek Hampton, sporting at least five bullet holes in a tight pattern centered on his chest, and a spaced out, near catatonic Sheila Hampton in a corner of the living room, her gaze locked on her husband's dead form and her body coiled tight enough to induce muscle cramps. When they managed to coax her out of her corner, the assembled officers got their first clear look at what had caught Derek's eye a few years before.

Twenty-three at the time, Sheila Hampton was all blonde hair, full curves and wistful blue eyes, barely held together by the filmy pink negligee she wore, and even less barely held together by a rapidly disintegrating nervous control.

At first able to utter little more than vague, inarticulate gutterals, it was only sometime later that she managed to explain that Derek had called her about an hour before, saying he would be home soon, and she'd decided to greet his arrival in a romantic way, so to speak. All of this ruined by an intruder who'd come in the door right behind Derek, gunned him down, then fled without as much as a glance at Sheila.

The cops back then hadn't bought her story for a second, and four months later neither did a jury. Carson County had a new assistant DA, Robert Harris, who'd come to town after serving for a few years in St. Louis, and the prosecution of Sheila Hampton was his first big case. Over the course of a six-day trial, Harris had eviscerated any possible defense that Sheila and her lawyer could devise, and it took the jury all of three hours to convict her.

In reality, as most observers pointed out, there was literally no physical evidence, other than her proximity to the body, to connect Sheila to the killing. Regardless, by the time Harris was through with her, the jury saw Sheila as a twisted combination of Jezebel, Delilah and Bonnie Parker.

I wasn't living in Providence at the time. Barely twenty-one years old, I'd made the move to St. Louis, hoping to break into the pro wrestling scene. I'd gotten hired on with the MWL, the Midwest Wrestling League, at the time serving mainly as a gopher for the owners. The last thing I was interested in was some boring court case from back home, but my mother, like most of Providence, followed it religiously and every time I talked to her, she'd fill me in on the latest developments.

From what I understood, the old-fashioned courtroom sketch artists went to town with that trial, so much so that some of their pictures almost came off as caricatures. One that I remembered my mom clipping out and sending to me showed Sheila Hampton sitting at the defense table, overblown almost to the point of looking like a modern-day Marilyn Monroe, complete with cleavage nearly down to her belly button, and the two siblings sitting in the front row on the prosecution side, glaring daggers at the little hussy.

The judge sentenced Sheila Hampton to life, with the possibility of parole in thirty years, and the case was closed. Until, that is, a few months back. A privately funded defendant advocacy group out of Kansas City, Missouri, who called themselves Amendment V had taken an interest in Sheila's case and her continued, nearly a quarter century later, protestations of innocence.

Few people had ever heard of Amendment V. Originally set up by a multi-millionaire from Olathe, Kansas, ten full-time employees, a host of volunteers, and certain select citizens who sat on their board comprised the group.

Kenneth Tamish, the rich guy who initially founded the organization, had made it big in both cattle and oil, then retired at the age of fifty to watch both his money and his family grow. That family had been disrupted several years later when his oldest girl, who'd bounced in and out of trouble with the law for most of her life, had ended up the defendant in a capital murder case, accused of killing one of her long-time friends in a dispute over a guy.

Tamish had hired enough lawyers to get her off, even with strong evidence indicating her guilt, only for his daughter, six months after successfully beating the rap, to confess on tape. In the swirl of publicity, Tamish found himself the odd man out in KC society because of using his wealth to get an admitted killer off, granted one of his own blood.

To expiate for his perceived complicity, some said, or to pull off a good PR stunt, others believed, he set up Amendment V, dedicated to scouring the Midwest for, and hopefully exonerating, falsely imprisoned people.

A couple of their people came to town, did some cursory interviews (very cursory considering the length of time since the original crime), then went up to the Eastern Correctional Center outside of Vandalia to interview Sheila.

One of the odd things about the Hampton case was that, considering the severity of the sentence, in the entire span of time since her conviction Sheila Hampton had not received a single appellate hearing. It was as if, once they'd put her away, the entire system, even her own lawyer, forgot about her. Supposedly, when Amendment V came along they were the first people to take a serious look at her case in all that time.

The do-gooder organization must have found something because they somehow managed to get an emergency hearing in front of the state appeals court and, not too long after, the appellate court overturned her conviction and ordered a new trial, at least nominally setting Sheila free after over two decades of incarceration.

Exactly six days later, Bernie Lyman sauntered into my gym and offered me some work.

"WHAT NEWS?" I ASKED.

"You've heard of Robert Harris, right?"

"Sure. The DA who prosecuted Hampton back when. So what?"

"Former prosecutor." Bernie's eyes were practically dancing in their sockets. "He made quite the splash for the Hampton trial, eventually made it up to Executive Assistant, then retired a few years back."

"Wasn't he a sure thing for the top job at some point?" I asked.

Bernie shrugged. "Everyone thought so, but he never went for it."

"What's your point?"

"The point, my boy, is that six days ago Sheila's conviction was overturned, the conviction brought about, primarily, through the efforts of former ADA Harris."

"Uh huh." I felt a sinking feeling in my gut that I was about to hear something bad.

"And this morning, Sheila was arrested for Harris's murder."

CHAPTER THREE

BERNIE HAD STOPPED BY MY GYM on the way to his first meeting with his new client. After we talked things over a bit more, I offered to help him out with the case in return for free legal advice down the line. Bernie, ever the pragmatist, no doubt thought I had in mind an open-ended commitment, and instead offered to hire me per diem at twice my usual rate.

Oh well, it was worth a shot, though I'd been hoping for that open commitment from him.

I stopped to talk to Lisa, who'd wrapped up her spin class a few minutes before, and told her I'd be indisposed for some time to come.

"How long?" she asked between swigs of a water bottle.

"Unsure," I replied. "May only be a few days. Could be quite a bit longer."

"Okay," she said. "I'll give a call if I need anything."

Without another word, she went off to get ready for her next class. The truth is, more and more Lisa's running the entire show. While I still do the paperwork, most of the time, and give the final word on any major decisions, Lisa's the one who's becoming the face of the business.

When I first met her, she was in a pretty bad place. She co-owned a vegetarian café with a boyfriend who abused her on a regular basis, while at the same time flirting with every one of their clients who gave him the time of day, leaving Lisa with the self-esteem of a dirty sponge. She wandered into my gym looking to improve herself, hoping in that way to keep the lout's eyes and hands from wandering.

About two months into her time as a client, she came in one day doing her best, though failing miserably, to cover up the bruises from the night before.

By that point, I'd gotten to know Lisa well enough that I couldn't let it go, so I went to visit said boyfriend to have a man-to-man talk. Although he was a fairly fit, athletic guy, my height, weight and full head of blond hair (even with the threads of gray), along with an outfit that made me look like an over-the-hill biker, allowed me to convince him to let Lisa off the hook.

Unfortunately, that left her with no job and nowhere to live. I gave her a job and provided for her to live for a while in a little room above the gym, and bit by bit she got back on her feet to the point that she was now practically running the gym and getting ready to invest in a home of her own.

Regardless of how long the job took, The Blaster would be in good hands until I returned.

Bernie and I climbed into my cashmere pearl Jeep Cherokee and headed to the downtown police station. Providence only has the one main station, with a few smaller facilities in troubled parts of the town, and it didn't take us long to find the room where Sheila Hampton was being held. At first, I had expected us to go to the county jail, but Bernie nixed that.

"The crime's only a few hours old, from what I heard," he said as I pulled the Cherokee into a slot in the parking garage right across the street from the station. "At the time I got the heads up, she was being interrogated."

"Don't you think you're jumping the gun at bit, pardon the expression?" I asked.

"In what way?"

"In hiring me to help. Maybe she won't even be charged."

Bernie shook his head. "I've already checked with the DA's office. Even in this short of a time, they think they have enough."

I shut off the car and turned to face him. "In a few hours? They can't even be done processing the crime scene."

"From what I hear they aren't."

"Then what's the rush?"

"That's why I need you, Blondie. Turns out they've already found the murder weapon, about a hundred feet away from the house, and it has Sheila's prints on it. Something's not right here. Now let's go inside and see our new client."

My instincts started to tingle. Something was off about Bernie. He's usually exuberant, but by now I was getting a false feeling about it. As if he were acting a part.

I felt eyes on me as we entered the ground floor of the central station. Most times, I could walk in here on business and feel perfectly at ease. I know a lot of people on the force. My PI work has brought me into contact with several over the years, and quite a few of the men and women on the force work out at the gym. Until recently, entering the building had always felt like coming onto friendly territory.

Didn't feel that way now. Earlier in the year, a sergeant on the force, Josh Nichols, and I had helped uncover some fairly hefty corruption in the department. Lieutenant Phil Kronberg, the head of the main detective division, turned out to be in bed with a local mob boss. More than just looking the other way or passing on information, Kronberg eventually became involved in a kidnapping and some attempted murders.

The whole incident had left a stink that hadn't yet dissipated. Even though Nichols and I had been cleared, and Nichols himself received a commendation, I was the civilian who'd helped bring down a cop. Corrupt through and through, true, but still a cop. I could understand some residual discomfort directed my way and only hoped it would ease over time.

And in case I thought I was just being paranoid, Bernie dispelled any possibility of that before we were even fifty feet in the building.

"We're getting a lot of stares," he whispered to me.

I nodded without saying anything back.

"Don't think it's all on you," he said. Bernie had represented me for the few days that I'd been under suspicion on the Lt. Kronberg and Paddy O'Brien case. "We're here to represent someone accused of killing someone they almost consider one of their own. Naturally, they're going to look at us a little suspiciously."

I didn't quite agree with that. By this time we'd made it to the front desk, and I held back any reply till we were alone again. Bernie spoke with the desk sergeant for a second, received a couple of nods in return, then motioned me his way.

"She's in room three up on the second floor. You ready?"

"Let's do it."

The two of us got on an elevator. Had I been alone, I would have taken the stairs, anything to help with the squats, but Bernie never met a staircase he didn't hate.

The door to room three was closed when we arrived, and I grabbed Bernie's arm before we went in.

"Shouldn't Nichols be around here somewhere?" I asked.

"How come?"

"Well, if this is as high profile as you say, why wouldn't a sergeant be handy?"

Bernie frowned. "I asked about him downstairs. Turns out he's down overseeing the crime scene."

"Well," I said, "at least they don't have him chained to a desk as some sort of punishment."

"Don't be too sure about that, Sam."

"Huh?"

"If you were an up and coming young detective, would you want to be handed this hot potato?"

I mulled that one over for a minute. I'd been feeling more uneasy by the moment. Bernie didn't wait for me to feel better. Without knocking, he turned the knob and entered the interrogation room, almost flourishing as he did so.

Just like they do on *Law and Order* reruns.

It seems that, no matter how new the building or modern the city, police interrogation rooms look the same everywhere. Small, usually barely enough space for more than two people to move around in. No windows, for obvious reasons, and furniture that looks as if it was rejected by Goodwill.

This one was no different. From the tan-colored chairs and table to the grimy floor and the beige walls, if you've seen one you've seen them all.

As expected, the room held three people. Two detectives, named Dawson and Thomkins, were standing, one next to the table and the other by the window. And a woman already attired in an orange jumpsuit was sitting at the table, her back to the door.

Det. Julie Dawson is a tall black woman, somewhere around the mid-thirties range. In excellent shape, she stands about five eight in her stocking feet. She comes into The Blaster every now and then, usually in the early morning before her shift, and puts herself through a cardio routine that makes an old hand like me sweat just to watch it.

The other detective, Lewis Thomas, I didn't know all that well. If Dawson is as far from the stereotyped image of a plainclothes cop as you can get, Thomas is the thing itself. Mid height, balding (for Chrissakes, the man wears a combover in the twenty-first century) and with about three inches of gut hanging over his belt. The two of them together make quite a contrast in styles.

Neither of them looked happy when Bernie and I breezed in. Well, Bernie breezed. I just walked in like a normal person.

"That's it boys and girls, time to wrap this up," my pal the lawyer said. "You've had all the time you're going to get out of her, at least until we get some ground rules worked out."

The two cops glared at us for a minute, then Dawson raised her hands in a submissive gesture. "Okay by me, she hasn't told us anything useful anyway."

Thomas continued frowning at the two of us but followed his partner's lead as she walked out. He was pulling the door shut when Bernie glanced back their way.

"Oh, by the way, detectives. Let's make sure you turn off anything that may allow you to listen in, okay?"

Thomas slammed the door shut. Bernie grinned as wide as I'd ever seen him do although my gut roiled a bit. As small as the Providence force is, I couldn't see the upside in ticking the cops off. I could only hope that when things finally shook themselves out the professionals on the force would realize I was only doing a job.

Yeah, right.

Bernie sat down in front of Sheila Hampton, whose back was still turned to me. I decided to give the two of them some space unless I was called on and leaned against the wall, arms crossed. The lawyer and his client huddled together for a few minutes. Even with only the three of us in the room, they spoke in whispers, as if Bernie didn't trust the cops not to listen in. It gave me a chance to check the accused woman out.

Once upon a time, Sheila Hampton had supposedly been a knockout. Long blonde hair, curves in all the right places, legs that went on forever, as my grandpa used to say. The woman sitting before me possibly, if you squinted just right, retained some of those traits, in modified form. However, from the slumped shoulders, brittle hair and sunken cheeks, two and a half decades in prison had clearly left their mark on her.

Go figure.

She shifted a bit, allowing me to see that they'd handcuffed her to the table.

After a short time of hushed talking, Bernie and Sheila leaned back in their chairs.

"Who's he?" Sheila Hampton said, pointing at me.

"This is Sam Quinton, my investigator. I've employed him to help us in this matter."

"You mean like a detective?"

"Yes," Bernie replied.

Sheila squinted at me for a minute. "He looks like a bouncer who had a rough night."

"Wrestler, actually," I put in. "Long ago. I've also done some nightclub bouncing in my time as well."

"A wrestler? Jesus Christ, Mr. Lyman. What kind of freak show are you putting on here?"

I shifted a bit against the wall and thought about whether to respond.

"Sheila, Mr. Quinton's been a professional investigator for several years. Believe me, he's as effective a man as we could have."

She looked me over for a second, then turned back to Bernie. "You actually think you're going to need some muscle on this thing?"

"It's possible," Bernie replied. "After all, if you didn't kill Harris—"

"I didn't, goddammit!"

"Then there's some reason someone wants to frame you. They have the gun they believe killed him, and they already have your prints on it. If you're telling me the truth, there's no way to avoid it. Someone wants to put you away again."

"How could they have done this?"

As the two of them continued talking, I cudgeled my brain over that question. I went with the assumption for the moment, although I wasn't convinced yet myself, that Sheila hadn't killed Robert Harris. If the gun supposedly found a short distance from his house was the murder weapon, and the forensics lab would have that pinned down quick enough, how could someone have possibly gotten her prints on it?

There was only one answer I could think of, and I didn't like it one bit.

Since Bernie Lyman was no fool, I was pretty sure he had figured the possibility as well.

A few minutes later, the two of them wrapped up their business. Bernie stood up and motioned to me that he was ready to go. Before leaving, he placed his hand on his client's shoulder and gave her a reassuring squeeze.

"You're not alone in this Sheila, not even close. Sam and I are going to get you through this."

Sam wasn't entirely sure he was on board yet, but it didn't seem the time to bring that up. Sheila swiveled in her chair, as far as the handcuffs on her wrists would let her and looked me over.

"You don't say much do you?" she asked.

"Only when I'm trying to outtalk the bad guys."

She frowned, obviously not a fan of flippancy, and after a moment shook her head and turned away.

"I'm trusting you, Mr. Lyman. I can't go back to prison, no matter what. Even if they get this fucked up charge to stick, can't they just say the time I served counts for something and let me go?"

Bernie smiled in a reassuring manner. "Hang in there, Sheila. We're only getting started."

CHAPTER FOUR

A MINUTE LATER WE WERE OUT THE BUILDING and headed toward the parking garage, Bernie's expression a lot more somber than before.

We walked in silence for a few seconds before I decided to break into his concentration.

"The prints," I said.

Bernie didn't reply, his gaze focused mainly on the ground as we walked.

"There's only two possibilities," I prodded.

He stopped and lifted his gaze up.

"Actually, I count three."

I started ticking off scenarios on my fingers. "One, it's her gun and someone got hold of it and used it to kill Harris."

Bernie frowned. "That's a bit preposterous, don't you think? She's been out of jail less than a week and already knew how to acquire a handgun?"

"Maybe." I ticked off a second finger. "Some kind of shenanigans somewhere in the bowels of authority."

"Bowels of authority? I thought you jocks didn't know any words over one syllable."

"So sue me." In hindsight, not the best thing to say to a lawyer. "Besides, I was only a make-believe jock. And I spent a lot of time on the road reading."

"Okay. But that's only two. There's the third possibility."

"That she actually did it?"

He nodded, then continued walking.

"You believe that?" I asked as I hurried to keep up with him.

Bernie spends most of his days sitting at a desk and exercises about once a decade, usually after his doctor insists he do so. I should have been able to pace him without even trying. Instead, something had him as animated as if he'd been struck by lightning.

"I'm not sure if I believe anything yet, Sam. I've only had this case an hour or so. In the room, how did she impress you in terms of intelligence?"

"You mean the couple of seconds she talked to me without insulting me?"

"Yes."

We started climbing the stairs to the level where we'd parked my car.

"I don't know. About normal, I'd say. She didn't come across as a criminal mastermind, if that's what you're asking."

Bernie grunted, then went silent again until we got to my Cherokee.

"Let's assume for a minute it's a frame," he said. "After all, she just spent twenty-five years inside on a false charge. Why take the chance of going back in?"

"There's all sorts of possible answers to that, Bernie. You know them all as well as I do."

We slid into our seats, and I started up the ignition.

"Of course, I do," he continued. "But let's go with the frame for just a minute. The big question isn't how. That can be accomplished all sorts of ways. What's the big question?"

I placed my hands on the steering wheel, at ten and two, and stared out the windshield. We'd parked at one of the walls, and through a space in front of me I could look out onto part of downtown Providence. In a café across the street, a young brunette woman wearing black pants and white uniform shirt was putting out a display easel for passersby.

I squinted. Today's special was roast beef au jus. I'd eaten at the place several times, and their roast beef was okay, though I wouldn't call it the best.

I remembered that I hadn't had breakfast yet.

"Why?" I asked.

"Exactly. If someone is framing her, why? For what possible reason. Even if someone out there wanted to kill Robert Harris, what's the benefit in going to the trouble of framing Sheila? What would they get out of it?"

I shifted into gear and began backing out.

"The 'why' is going to have to wait," I said.

"Huh?"

"We need to figure out the 'how' first, and that will point us in the direction of 'who.'"

Bernie began smiling again. "And the 'who' will tell us the 'why.'"

I grunted as I began negotiating the winding turns necessary to exit the garage.

"And now," Bernie continued, "you know why I need you."

"Part of it," I said. "How about you give me the rest of it?"

He looked sideways at me but didn't say anything. After a few seconds, I decided I had to prod.

"Bernie, if you were an Indian your animal totem would be the turtle. You're probably the most careful, step-watching person I know. Yet ever since you came in my place this morning you've acted like you have a live wire down your pants. You want to tell me why?"

"It could be a major case," he said, a slightly defensive whine in his voice.

"Sure," I said, "just like all the other major cases you get on a semi-annual basis. What's so special with this one?"

He turned away and stared out the windshield. By this time, we'd exited the garage and were headed back towards his office. I was going to drop him off and go visit the crime scene to see what crumbs I could come up with. Maybe grab a breakfast sandwich on the way. However, I didn't want to do that until I had a better idea of just what I was getting into.

"Landon," he finally said.

"Huh?"

"Howard Landon. Look it up if you want to, but I doubt you'll get the whole story. And pardon me if I don't really feel like talking about it."

Glancing out of the side of my eye, I noticed a shiny tightness I'd never before seen on the rumpled lawyer's face. In the few seconds since I'd last looked at him, his cheeks were practically glistening.

I let it go as I pulled into an open slot at the curb in front of his building. Despite his manic act of a while earlier, something was bothering Bernie big time. He exited the Cherokee and, without even a wave, headed into his building.

CHAPTER FIVE

A BOUT TWENTY MINUTES LATER, I wheeled down one of the oldest residential streets in town. You can always tell the older streets in Providence because they're the ones with the largest and richest houses. When Bernie had given me the address, I'd puzzled it a bit. As ADA, Robert Harris had had a high profile in local government but not one that would have rated this neighborhood.

All I knew about him was that a few months after the Hampton trial he'd been promoted up to Executive ADA, one rung below the top slot, and stayed there the rest of his career. Judging by the neighborhood, that didn't quite compute. Someone of his rank would have been paid well, though not quite that well.

Then again, beyond the basics I didn't know that much about the guy. His wife could have been well off, or maybe there was old family money. I put it out of my head for the moment and concentrated on more immediate issues.

I didn't have to bother checking house numbers because at the end of the second block I saw a plethora of official vehicles, huddled bystanders and yellow crime scene tape.

Kind of puzzling to see that much activity. The crime had taken place over twelve hours before, with the suspect arrested only a few hours later. Then I spotted, about a hundred yards down the street, a cluster of news vans from our three local stations.

All in all, it looked like a pretty good show.

The street itself had been opened up some time before, and I meandered the Cherokee past the house, looking for a particular face among the official presence. I could have simply buzzed him on his cell, but if he were too busy he'd ignore the call.

I got lucky. I had made it almost past the house when, in my rearview mirror, I saw Josh Nichols coming out the front door. I slowed down for a moment, to make sure he'd see me, then sped up and took a right at the corner. I parked alongside a blue two-story house with gray trim and only had to wait a few minutes before the passenger door of the Cherokee opened up.

"Tell me this is a coincidence," Nichols said as he settled into the seat.

"No such luck, buddy."

"Crap."

Although Nichols and I had both grown up around the Providence area, we had never met until we both moved to St. Louis. I was performing for the Midwest Wrestling League and he was a patrolman with the SLPD. To make ends meet, he would sometimes do security at our live shows, and the two of us developed an acquaintance.

We lost touch for a while when, approaching forty, I had my chance to move up to the big time. More or less concurrently, Nichols moved back to Providence to care for his ailing mother and got a job with the local cops, quickly moving into the detective bureau.

My tenure in the big time didn't last more than six months. Blowing out the same knee three times will pretty much end a career, and I ended up going into bouncing and light security work. This eventually transitioned into preparing for a private investigator's license, in the midst of which I inherited the gym from an old buddy and moved back to Providence.

Somehow or other, I'd gone from having no job prospects to owning two businesses, while Nichols eventually became a detective sergeant.

"It's been a while," I said, glancing sideways at my friend. He doesn't look like a cop, more like an accountant or salesman. On the other hand, he's only thirty-two, and you can already see the worry lines developing.

"Well, you know," Nichols said. "The new boss's taking some getting used to."

I didn't know how to answer that. After the Kronberg debacle, Nichols had been the obvious person to move up to detective lieutenant, and for a few weeks there it looked like a sure thing. Then, someone high up in the city government took a second look at the situation and overruled Nichols's promotion.

In a way, I could see their reasoning. Taking out the guy above you and moving into his slot doesn't exactly endear you to your fellow cops, no matter how corrupt said guy above may have been. I figured that walking through the central station today as I had, feeling all those stares, was only a fraction of what he'd encountered.

"If it's not coincidence, what's the deal? You working with Lyman on this?"

"Maybe," I said. "Figured I'd check with you and see just how bad it is."

"For the Hampton woman? Pretty damned bad. I suppose Lyman told you the basics."

"He said that Harris arrived home sometime after seven last night, and a little after eight a neighbor called 911, reporting what sounded like a gunshot."

"Actually three. And the patrol unit showed up to find the guy dead in his living room, shot at close range."

I drummed my fingers on the steering wheel as I ran the time.

"That doesn't add up Josh. How'd you guys get onto Sheila Hampton so quick?"

Nichols cast a hooded glance my way.

"Car looks good," he said. "How'd you get all those bullet holes patched?"

My former Cherokee had been damned near obliterated in a drive by shooting.

"You need to sharpen up your powers of observation, buddy. The insurance agent took one look at the damage and wrote the whole thing off. This is a replacement."

Nichols shook his head. "And you went out and got the same

model and color? What the hell happened to The Blond Bomber, the wrestling champ who always lived the high life?"

"He grew old and retired," I replied, "and stop changing the subject. What made you guys glom onto Hampton right away?"

"Despite the fact that she has an A-number one motive? Other than that, I'm not saying anything, Sam. Jillian Hirschoff is going to do all the talking on this one, both for public consumption and otherwise."

I thought about that one. Hirschoff had been the First Assistant DA for a few years now. Something this high profile, you'd expect the DA himself to take the reins, at least in public. And maybe he would eventually. I guessed he was waiting to see which direction the wind blew.

"Come on, Josh. If I'm working for Bernie, he's going to get the low down eventually anyway. Why not cough it up now?"

"Because we're on different sides of the fence this time, guy. And on a more practical level, you have any idea how many eyes are on me waiting for me to screw up again?"

"You were cleared on Kronberg."

Nichols shook his head, making me feel like the dumb kid in class.

"Just because most of the city's cops work out at your place, Sam, doesn't mean you hear everything going down. Far as that goes, you're talking the police force."

"Yeah?"

Nichols reached down and grasped the door handle. "I'm talking City Hall. Phil Kronberg may not have had a whole lot of personal friends over there, but we'll be unearthing Paddy's chits for some time to come."

A dull heaviness settled in my gut. The late Paddy O'Brien had been an Irish immigrant who somehow made his way to mid Missouri and basically took over all the rackets in the area. At least, that's what almost everyone thought until earlier in the year, when the war between KC and St. Louis revealed that Paddy, far from being his own man, had merely served all those years as a figurehead for the St. Louis don. Providence and the surrounding area is such a small community, in relative terms, that the idea of rampant corruption had never occurred to me.

I was beginning to realize just how much Nichols had risked by coming out to meet me.

"You going to be okay?" I asked my friend.

"I will as long as no one spots me sitting here chatting with you. Do me a favor and don't come around asking for any help, okay? Actually, if I were you, I'd steer clear of Bernie Lyman entirely until this is over."

"Why?" I asked. "Somebody after Bernie too?"

Nichols peered at me. "Nothing like that, as far as I know. It's just that I'd guess this whole thing's a little too personal for him."

"Come again?"

"He and the Hampton woman's original lawyer were tight. Thought you knew that."

"I did. So?"

"Maybe Bernie isn't looking at this whole thing too objectively."

CHAPTER SIX

I MADE MY WAY BACK TO THE GYM and after chatting with Lisa for a few minutes went into my office. I spent some time on the computer, dug up enough to give me the basic blueprint I was looking for, then left again and headed back across town, hoping to catch Bernie in his office.

Lyman & Associates sits on the top floor of a downtown building, or what passes for downtown in Providence. In the case of his building, the top floor was actually the second, and you won't find any buildings downtown more than five stories tall. The ground floor held a Chinese restaurant, with the second floor divided between Bernie's office and a low-wattage public radio station. What the location lacked in impressiveness it made up for in convenience, seeing as it was only two and a half blocks from the county court house.

I walked up his stairs about eleven thirty and lucked out. Bernie sat behind his desk, the desk itself covered with the makings of a sub sandwich, chips and dessert from a store about half a block away.

"Bit early for lunch, isn't it?" I asked.

I'd caught him in mid bite, and he chewed for a second before swallowing a chunk of Reuben.

"Hampton arraignment is at one straight up."

I frowned at that.

"Doesn't that seem a little quick?" I asked. "They only arrested her this morning."

Bernie took another bite from his sandwich.

"It's definitely a cause for concern. Now, what'd you manage to find out?"

I told him about my run in with Nichols.

"Well, Christ, Blondie, why do you think I hired you? I thought sure you'd be able to dig something up for me."

I shook my head in exasperation.

"Bernie, quit the bullshit, okay? You know Nichols almost as well as I do, and you knew damned good and well he wasn't going to spill anything on an ongoing investigation, especially one as potentially explosive as this. Why don't you stop screwing around and tell me exactly what you expect me to do for you. Otherwise, pay me for my time, and I'll go back and help Lisa run the gym."

"I thought what I expected was obvious. I want you to investigate for me."

"You've never needed me before," I said. "Why now? You planning on playing Perry Mason or something? Or is all of this about Howard Landon?"

Bernie frowned for a second, then moved his food to the side.

"You looked it up?" he asked.

"No matter what you may think, Bernie, you don't owe anyone anything. Least of all a man who's been dead for over twenty years."

"Says you," Bernie said.

"That's right, says I. What are you doing here, man? Working off some sort of martyr complex?"

"I'm trying to make things right."

"Right for who? Sheila Hampton? You? Or your mentor?"

Bernie wiped his lips with his napkin, stood up and walked over to the window. He stood looking down at the street, and when he began talking it was almost as if he were talking to himself rather than me.

"Okay, here's the thing," he said, his tone a lot more serious than it had been. "You were right that this seems to be moving fast. I agree, and I don't think it's just because of who the victim or the accused is."

"Meaning what?"

"Meaning I've got the feeling there's something more going on here. Something rather deep."

"Just now?" I asked.

"Huh?"

"Something deeper just now. Or does this go all the way back to the beginning?"

He stared at me, and I don't think I've ever seen such pain in a man's eyes as I saw in Bernie's right then.

I stared back at him for a moment and decided to ask the question I hadn't yet asked.

"Is she guilty, Bernie?"

The lawyer turned back, his eyes focused on me.

"You're assuming I asked her. That I wanted to know."

"I am. Did you?"

Bernie rolled his head, popping his neck.

"It's a question you don't always ask a client, Sam."

"Especially when you don't want to know the answer."

He nodded, his eyes never leaving me. After a moment of no response, I asked again.

"Did you?"

"Yes, I did. She says she didn't."

"She has one hell of a motive. According to the appellate court, there's a good chance she's been away for over twenty years on a wrongful conviction," I said.

Bernie shook his head. "Not exactly. What they said was that she had grounds for appeal that have been denied all these years. As far as I'm concerned, she was put away on a bum rap."

"Did Howard Landon think so?"

Bernie sighed and sat back down in his chair. He placed his forearms on his desk and slumped half forward.

"I'm not sure what Howard thought back then. He brought me in as second chair with only a week to go until trial, said he needed another warm body to impress the jury with his stature. Or something like that. I figured he just wanted me to get trial experience. He'd been talking about retiring for a couple of years."

"And by the time you came along, all of the preliminary discussions between Howard and Sheila had already taken place."

Bernie wasn't looking at me, or probably at anything in the

office. He stared at the wall, and I had the sense he was gazing into the far past.

"In hindsight, I'm pretty sure he thought her innocent. You have to understand, Sam. Howard Landon was the toughest, most in-your-face attorney I'd ever met."

"One who just happened to help you pay for law school after your parents died," I said.

He blinked at that, coming back at least momentarily to the present. "You really did do your homework, didn't you?"

"You hired me to investigate."

He leaned back in his chair and stared directly at me.

Back in the present.

"Yes, Howard helped me get through law school. And threw me odd jobs here and there my first year out of the gate to keep me eating. I'm sure he would've liked to bring me on as an associate, but he never had more than a one-man practice."

"Sheila Hampton," I prodded. "Why do you think he thought her innocent?"

"Because I've never seen him fight so hard for any client as he did for her. He put on the most mind-blowing defense you've ever seen. If you were to go back and look at the original transcripts, you'd see just how many holes he managed to poke in the prosecution's case."

His voice faltered a bit at the end.

"And all for nothing," I said.

"The jury came back in barely thirty minutes, guilty on all counts."

"Was the fix in?" I asked.

He leaned back, and I got the feeling he was about to pull away from me again.

"Bernie," I almost shouted. "Did you or Howard think the fix was in on that trial?"

"Howard did. And I think that's what killed him. He had his first heart attack barely two weeks later."

"Was it that bad?" I asked.

"All of his motions squashed," Bernie continued, "all his objections overruled. Yet he made Harris and his team look like clowns."

"Except they got the conviction," I pointed out.

Bernie frowned, though he didn't say anything in response.

"Why'd she just get out now, Bernie? Why no appeals back then?"

He blanched. "That was always kind of confusing. Trust me, much as I thought of Howard, there was plenty of room for reversible errors. I thought sure some enterprising attorneys would take her case on, but no one ever did."

"Why didn't Landon? If he had that much material to go with . . ."

Bernie frowned, and I had the feeling he'd wondered the same thing over the years.

"I asked him about that once. It wasn't like him to just let a client drop. But he always blew my questions off, and it wasn't too long after that he threw in the towel and quit practicing. Said losing such a big case had taken away his drive."

Now it was my turn to frown. "'Course, he was getting up in years, right? It may have only been natural for him to retire?'

"Sure. It seemed that way . . ." Bernie spread his hands in frustration.

"What about you?" I asked. "Fixing a case like that could have jumpstarted your career."

Bernie squirmed. "I considered it a time or two, but it just didn't feel right. Going against Howard, even if second hand."

"Everyone, including her own lawyer, just gave up on Sheila?" I asked.

"That's about it."

"Until Amendment V showed up and made a case for incompetent counsel. Do you think that's right?" I asked.

Bernie stared down at his desk. "I didn't see it that way at the time, but I was too young, too green. I've thought it over a lot since then, especially since she's back in the news, and yeah, despite the show he put on I wondered every now and then if Howard may have thrown the trial."

I wanted to say something, but didn't know any words that would make this mess sound right. After a minute, Bernie glanced back up at me.

"That's why I have to help her now, Sam. If Howard did something to that girl, if he in some way let her down, I've got to make it right."

CHAPTER SEVEN

COURTROOM FIVE OF THE CARSON COUNTY COURTHOUSE was packed at one that afternoon. PI work takes me in and out of the courthouse on occasion, so while I'm not a regular I am more familiar with the layout than the average citizen. Even on big local cases, such as bank robberies, rapes and murders, you rarely see a courtroom more than half full. Seeing Room Five at standing room only was a bit of a shock.

I figured I wouldn't have gotten in at all if Bernie hadn't left word downstairs that I was part of the Hampton defense team. The bailiff who checked me in, a short black man with salt and pepper hair and a bit of a beer gut, scowled at me. Professional to the end, he kept quiet although the look on his face made his feelings clear.

I considered giving him a spiel about the Constitution and pre-sumption of innocence, but figured it would only annoy the people waiting in line behind me. After he checked me down and gave me a plastic-coated clip to grant me access, I started to walk on when he couldn't keep his tongue any longer.

"If you're going to work for a murderer, the least you could do is get presentable for court."

Again, I thought of replying, then decided not to. Obviously, Robert Harris had been fairly well liked around the courthouse, even though he'd been retired for years, which would only make Bernie's job even more difficult.

Besides, the guy had a point. Sketchers, Levi's and an untucked black tee-shirt aren't exactly proper court-wearing apparel. At least, at the tail end of summer, I wasn't wearing my cracked black leather jacket.

I managed to get a seat in the far-left corner of the courtroom and sat back to watch the proceedings unfurl. Several members of the local media were sitting a few rows up from me, eager to record every word they could get. They'd been let in for the arraignment, but I had a feeling that if the time ever came for an actual trial either Bernie or the prosecutor would do their best to get them excluded, depending on how it fit with trial strategy.

Naturally, at first I focused most of my attention on the defense table. Bernie was there, along with Sheila Hampton and a female deputy guarding her. Sheila looked different than she had when we'd seen her just a short while before. Meeting with Bernie and me at the jail she'd been defensive, naturally wary of trusting in anyone.

Now, confronted head on with the majesty of the criminal justice system that had already chewed her up once, she appeared downright defiant. Glaring around the room, yet locking eyes with no one, she almost had a snarl on her face. She almost reminded me of Jimmy Cagney daring the world to come get him.

After noting the principal players in place, I did what Bernie was paying me to do and began scanning the various people crowded into the spectator section of the room. If Sheila hadn't killed Harris, then someone had done a damned good job of framing her in a matter of only hours. That denoted planning, not to mention resources, which presented a two-fold question. Who could do it and who would want to? It was less than fifty-fifty that the hypothetical real killer would show up at the arraignment, but no matter how low, it was worth a shot to scope the proceedings out.

Both Bernie and Jillian Hirschoff, a tall, slender redhead in a tailored green pants suit, were standing, with the Assistant DA making the first pitch. I pretty much assumed there was no way in hell Sheila would get bail. I ignored them and continued scanning the crowd.

Besides the media, the largest number of people packed into the courtroom fit a type. Over sixty, more or less equally split between male and female, with a good number of them working on crossword puzzle books. These were your traditional court watchers, the stereotypical retired individual with nothing better to do during the day.

Across from me, in the back row on the other side of the room, sat a cluster of five women perched forward in their seats, their eyes locked on the proceedings. They all looked to be in the forty to fifty-year age range, with teased, 1980's style hairdos and tight-fitting clothes. I wondered if by chance they were friends of Sheila's from back when, come to either show their support or, more cynically, bask in a moment of catty superiority.

My life may not be great, but at least I didn't end up like poor Sheila over there.

No matter how hard I looked, I didn't see anybody wearing a top hat while twirling his mustache, no old geezer wearing a thousand-dollar suit rubbing his hands together while cackling at the success of his plot, or a straight-laced government drone wearing a dark blue suit relieved that the planted evidence had worked.

I did, however, feel someone checking me out, and turned to look straight ahead. About two rows in front, a tall fiftyish woman with long blonde hair had her arm propped on the back of her seat, her body twisted enough to put me right in her line of sight.

Outside, she silently mouthed to me before turning back to watch the proceedings. I tuned into what was happening just as, as expected, the judge denied Sheila bail and ordered her held until trial.

As the deputy guarding her led Sheila away and Bernie walked over to speak to the prosecutor, I glanced over where the woman who'd motioned to me had been sitting. She was already up and half out of the courtroom, pausing only long enough to bat her eyes and nod her head towards the outer doors.

What the hell?

CHAPTER EIGHT

BECAUSE THE WOMAN DIDN'T LOOK FAMILIAR, I assumed she wasn't from the local media. Quite frankly, although I didn't have a clue who she was, unless it was a case of mistaken identity she knew me.

She was sitting on one of the benches arrayed along the outer edge of the lobby, which allowed me to get a better look at her as I approached. Not quite as tall as I'd first assumed, she topped out around five seven or so.

She wore a light gray skirt which looked, to my untrained eyes, to be made of silk, and a navy blazer over a maroon blouse. Her hair didn't quite get to her shoulders, though you wouldn't call it short, and on her wrist she wore what looked like a fairly expensive watch although I hadn't the remotest idea what brand.

Walking up to her, I noticed the hair wasn't quite as blonde as it had appeared in the overhead lights of the courtroom. In the sunlight coming through the windows, I could see a few streaks of gray here and there.

Kind of reminded me of my hair, and it somehow went nicely with her eyes, which I now saw were a fairly striking shade of green.

"Mr. Quinton," she said, holding out her hand. Having no clue as to her identity, I declined to shake.

She held the beat about three seconds, then glanced down at the unaccepted hand.

"So, okay," she said, her face showing no resentment. "I guess it's right to business."

"That depends," I said.

"On?"

"On who you are and what sort of business."

She laughed, the barest of giggles, before reaching into her purse and pulling out an embossed business card. I took it from her and looked it over.

"Karyn Roberts?" I asked. The card ID'd her as a Vice-President at Lewis and Cochran Public Relations, a firm out of KC Mo. Although I'd never had any dealings with the PR world, the name niggled at my memory.

"I don't think I need any public relations work," I said, "but I'll keep your card just in case."

Karyn Roberts shook her head, giving me a look as if I'd just flunked kindergarten.

"Mr. Quinton, I've only done PR work for the last ten years."

"Okay." Out of the corner of my eye, Bernie exited the court-room, spotted me, and headed my way.

"Before that," Ms. Roberts continued, "I was a reporter."

"And I'll bet," I said, the light finally coming, "that you spent some time working at our little home town paper."

Ms. Roberts grinned. "You'd be right," she said as Bernie came alongside of us, frowning at her. "And I think you and I need to talk. Call me."

Glancing briefly at Bernie, she stood up and walked away.

CHAPTER NINE

"**W**HO WAS THAT?" BERNIE ASKED, HIS eyes slitted. I handed him the card. He glanced it over and handed it back.

"You looking for a publicity agent?" he asked.

I frowned, unsure if he was mad specifically at me or the world in general. "I was kind of distracted in there," I said. "I'm guessing you didn't get Sheila bail?"

Bernie snorted and turned to head out the door. He didn't speak until we'd made it to the sidewalk.

"Took everything I had not to go off on the judge. That woman's been locked away for over half her life, and now in less than a week they're putting her back inside. You have any idea the kind of pressure that puts on me?"

"Doesn't do her much good either," I said.

He paused at the door of the parking garage and stared for a moment at his partial reflection in the glass.

"Good point," he said. "I'm guess I'm sounding like a grade-A jerk right about now, huh?"

He opened the door and we headed up to the third level, where we'd parked earlier. "Did you see anyone who looked hinky in there?"

"Bernie, no one says 'hinky' anymore, okay? Actually, no one ever said it."

He waved that away. "Did you?"

I shook my head. "Not really. Except for the sheer number, looked like a regular bunch of court watchers. More media than usual, but that's to be expected."

We made it to Bernie's car and slid inside. As close as his office is to the courthouse, we could have walked it, but Bernie had just bought a new Mercedes and liked to show it off.

We sat silent for a few minutes as I gave him time to mull things over. When five minutes had gone by, I'd had enough.

"How much do they have on Hampton?" I asked him.

"More than enough," he said while staring out the windshield. "The gun, a thirty-eight believe it or not, was found about half a block from the house. It has her prints on it, and the cops are scouring the gun shops looking for someone remembering the sale. She threatened to do Harris in plenty of times over the years, to anyone who would listen actually, and she doesn't have an alibi, says she was staying in her hotel room all night."

A cold wave washed over me.

"Bernie," I said, "have you ever heard of prints being run that fast?"

He turned from the window to look at me. "Nope. And I'm guessing neither have you."

It was my turn to mull things over. It didn't take long at all to do the simple math.

"Would you be surprised," I asked, "if they come up with some- one who remembers selling her the gun?"

"Actually," he replied, "I'd be pretty surprised if they didn't."

"Drive me back to your office," I said.

"Why?"

"So I can start earning what you're going to pay me."

CHAPTER TEN

DEPENDING ON YOUR POINT OF VIEW, Providence is either a small city or a large town. With a little over a hundred thousand year-round residents, it sits in almost the exact middle of the state. For nine months out of every year, when the university students show up, the population swells by between thirty and forty thousand. Not what one would call a roaring metropolis.

Even so, our large town/small city boasts a fairly upscale profile, with the main industries being education, health care and financial services. This allows the police force to possess services and capabilities that other small-city forces can't match.

When it comes to the intricate operations, such as DNA testing, they sometimes have to make use of the main state police crime lab, just down the highway about thirty miles in the state capital. However, for the more day-to-day demands, such as fingerprint identification, things can be handled in house.

The Crime Scene division, which includes the forensics people, is located on the second floor of the main PD building downtown. Seeing as I'd just been there with Bernie that morning, and received a less than cordial reception, I decided not to waltz back in to get the information I wanted.

I steered my car into a parking space across the street, a short jog down from the courthouse and pulled out my phone.

"Forensics, Paulson," a voice answered after only two rings.

"Hey, Paulie. It's Sam."

Reynard Paulson, who hates his first name enough that he always introduces himself as Paul or Paulie, actually groaned into the phone.

"No way, man."

I frowned. "You don't know what I'm going to . . ."

"If this is anything to do with the Hampton broad, the answer is no."

"Paulie," I said, "you're in your mid-thirties. You're not old enough to legitimately go around using the word 'broad.'"

"Doesn't matter how I talk, and don't change the subject like you always do. Whatever it is, the answer is no."

My frown deepened. If I didn't watch it, I'd end up with more wrinkles than my forty-six year old face already had.

"Paulie," I said, "I just need the answer to one question."

"No."

"It will take you ten seconds to tell me."

Several seconds of silence followed. I sat patiently, but found myself checking in my rearview mirrors. Maybe everyone's paranoia was rubbing off on me.

"I can't help you with anything man, not this time."

In the next instant, I was listening to dead air.

Putting my phone away, I sat and drummed my fingers on the dashboard for a few minutes. Although Paulson and I weren't super tight or anything, we'd both done favors for each other over the years. Around half a dozen times I'd come to him for help, and he'd always come through. By the same token, there'd been once or twice that he'd run into personal problems of one sort or another, and I'd helped him straighten them out.

Not best buds, and I doubted that either of us would take a bullet for the other, but we knew each other and got along okay. Now he was acting spacey in a way I'd never encountered.

Could be that Bernie was on to something.

I came to a quick decision, fired up the Cherokee and drove three blocks west and two north. Although I saw an open parking space directly in front of my destination, I passed it up and drove another two blocks before spotting an empty spot off of a side street. Turning off the ignition, I climbed out then walked back to my destination.

Jerry's Sandwich Shop doesn't make the best food in town, but it tastes decent and is a reasonable price. It's big attraction for me today was that the owner, Jerry, happens to be Paulie's cousin, and makes a habit, especially since Paulie's divorce, of comping his lunches. As a result, Paulie hits the shop almost every day right around two, after the lunch rush is over.

I didn't want to go in because Jerry and I know each other on a glancing basis. Plus, with the shop only seating about thirty people, it's kind of hard to be inconspicuous in there. There's an activewear shop next door with a large plate glass front.

I walked inside that shop, positioned myself next to a display of wet suits and waited.

Must have been a busy day at the office because twenty minutes later Paulie hadn't yet shown up, and one of the shop clerks, a red-headed guy around five seven or so, was giving me odd looks. With my size and appearance, I get a lot of people thinking I'm scoping out their place for a robbery.

The guy swallowed, his Adam's apple bobbing, and started my way. I shook my head and gave him the "Mr. Geniality" grin. It was one of the facial expressions from my time in the wrestling ring, one that showed the entire world that all I wanted in life was to be everyone's pal. I usually wore it right before I sucker punched some poor clod from behind and stole his girl.

The kid blanched and wobbled away.

Maybe I need to practice Mr. Geniality more.

Before I could worry about that too much, though, Paulie showed up, scurrying toward Jerry's for his mid-day sustenance. A tall, gangly guy who tops out around six foot and can't weigh over one sixty, he was moving fast, almost rushing, and I barely had time to leave the activewear shop and corner him on the street. As soon as he saw me he slowed down, his face tightening almost as much as the salesman's in the store I'd just left, and shifted his gaze back and forth, as if looking for a stage exit. His black hair, which always had the slightest bit of a greasy look to it, was tousled every which way on his head, the perfect complement to the straggly goatee on his chin

What the hell, I wondered. Was I giving off some sort of stench today?

Whatever, I was already a little tired of all the dancing around I'd dealt with from officialdom, and it wasn't even the end of the day yet. I didn't give Paulson a chance to back away, instead going straight at him like a bull, just like in the days when I targeted an opponent from across the ring and plowed right into them.

The difference was, I didn't intend to hurt Paulie, but I did want the guy to at least say something to me.

"I can't say anything to you, Blondie," were the first words out of his mouth.

So much for the brute interrogation technique.

"Come on, Paulie. There's just a few things I want to know. It's not going to get you in trouble or anything."

Paulson shook his head, and I had the impression he'd just realized we were talking on a public street with people moving back and forth all around us. His shoulders slumped, and he jerked his head towards the sub shop.

I followed him in and snagged one of the three empty tables while he went to the counter and picked up his order. He went right up to the side of the counter, and they handed him a tray full of food. Leading me to deduce that he'd called his order in ahead of time.

At least I was making some sort of investigative progress today.

A minute later he sat down in front of me and unwrapped a twelve-inch sandwich packed with salami, genoa and pepperoni, layered with at least five different cheeses and practically soaking in some sort of sauce. I tipped my head back and gave him a sharp look, wondering where the hell all of that was going to fit into his skinny frame.

"You eat like that every day and I'm going to have to discount you a membership to The Blaster," I said.

The lab tech, already chewing full out, shook his head. He took a drink of his soda.

"Ain't gonna happen, man. I weighed one fifty-five when I was eighteen and haven't put on a pound since."

Shrugging, I let the matter drop.

"The fingerprints on the Hampton case," I said.

Paulie shifted his gaze sideways again, then turned back to me. "Yeah, I knew that's what you were after. I'm telling you guy, you weren't in the building ten minutes, you and that lawyer, before everyone had the word."

"And what's the word?" I asked.

"Mum. Or mud, if you want it to apply to your name. It was made clear through the grapevine, very clear, that no one was to give you guys anything."

"There's a little problem with that on the legal side," I said. "It's called discovery."

By this point, Paulson had already made it almost halfway through his sandwich, and I had to sit and wait for him to finish masticating.

"Sure," he said when he came up for air. "They have to give the defense everything when they go to trial. At least, everything they can use. But what's to stop them from slow-walking the whole thing?"

"Like they slow walked the fingerprint ID on the gun?"

Pauslon stopped in mid chew, his gaze locked with mine.

"What can I tell you?" he asked after a second.

"You can tell me why a process that ordinarily would take several days at least took a couple of hours this time."

Paulson shook his head, looking at me as if he wondered if I'd ever fallen on my head as a kid.

"Come on, Quinton, you're not that slow. The lady capped a former DA, and even though he'd been out of the game for a while, Harris had plenty of friends. You think they're not going to rush that sucker as much as they can?"

I mused over that one for a while as Paulson finished his sandwich and began digging into the first of three chocolate chip cookies that had come with his meal. When he paused to take another drink, I stood up.

"One last thing, Paulie, then I'll take off. Have you heard any whispers about anything more going on here than just a speeded-up process?"

Paulson paused in mid cookie and thought that one over.

"You mean like some kind of frame or cover up?" he asked a few minutes later.

I nodded, watching his face. Once or twice over the years, he and I have ended up in the same card games together, and I knew that he didn't have much of a poker face.

"Naw," he said. "Haven't heard anything like that, just that they wanted everyone to hop right on this. Put out a message. You know what I mean?"

I knew what he meant, even though it didn't track. A man who hadn't worked in local government for years would still have lots of friends, as my buddy the lab tech had pointed out. But that everything would fall together that quick and neat?

Sure, I knew what Paulson meant.

I just wasn't buying it, at least not yet.

CHAPTER ELEVEN

I HAD SOME DOUBTS NIGGLING AT ME ABOUT THIS CASE, primarily about Bernie's involvement. He'd acted a little evasive as we'd left the arraignment hearing, and that, along with Nichols's comment earlier, pointed me in my next direction.

It was easier to get in to see Sheila Hampton the second time around. I'd figured it would be harder without Bernie in tow, and his absence did raise an eyebrow or two among the jail staff. Seeing the two of us together earlier, they knew I was part of Sheila's legal team and, Carson County law enforcement being the smallish community it is, the sergeant manning the visitor desk didn't see a problem with my meeting with her alone.

If he'd given me any grief, I would have offered him a six-month free membership to the gym.

Or maybe not. If I did so, Lisa would have given me hell. Anymore, she watched the gym's bottom line closer than I did.

They situated me in another of the drab, smallish interview rooms and asked me to wait for a few minutes. It was actually closer to ten minutes before the door opened, and a female jailer marched Sheila in.

When she looked at me, Sheila frowned and shook her head.

I waved her to a chair. She stood there for a moment, mouth downturned, before using her manacled hands to pull the hard tan chair out and sit down. The jailer glanced at me, shook her head, held up five fingers and left.

I was prepared for some difficulty, guessing that being denied bail would put Sheila in an even worse mood than earlier.

"What do you want?" she half grumbled.

I was wrong. Same pleasant, smiling Sheila.

"I wanted to talk to you without Bernie around," I said.

"Why? Isn't he your boss?"

While I preferred to think of myself as an independent contractor, I didn't see a reason to argue the point.

Mainly because an argument seemed to be what the woman wanted.

"I just get the feeling that you're not too comfortable around legal people."

"Any reason I should be? Tell me how you'd feel if you were sent away for half your life."

"Bernie's on your side."

"Yeah, and you can see what a great job he did. I'm here, aren't I? And everyone on the block's telling me what a hot-ass lawyer the guy is? Why should I believe any of you people?"

I spread my hands and gave her my softest grin. "Hey," I said, "I could have shown up here wearing a suit."

She gave me a closer look, then shook her head. "Okay. You don't look like the others."

"True."

"You look more like a bum."

Maybe I had to work on my professional appearance a bit. I decided to try another tack.

"If you distrust Bernie so much," I asked, "why'd you hire him?"

She gave me a different expression this time, one of almost disgust. I used to get almost the same look from my teachers in high school when I struggled with geometry.

Sheila glanced over at the door, her mouth still downturned into an almost snarl. I couldn't really blame the woman for being pissed at the whole world and had to work not to take the attitude personally.

"Just how far into this are you?" she asked. "I didn't hire Lyman. He came to me and offered his services."

"And you took him up just like that?"

She frowned even harder. "All those years inside, I'm not exactly rolling in dough. And I sure as hell didn't want to take my chance with a public defender if I could help it."

My brain was starting to whirl, and I wasn't entirely sure which way was up and which down.

"What about Amendment V?" I asked. "If they got you sprung, surely they had attorneys who would . . ."

"Oh, sure," she answered, shaking her head. "I called them first. They said it wasn't their kind of gig, and that they'd send someone over who knew this end of things better than they did."

I somehow doubted they used the term "their kind of gig," but let that slide as well. And from what little I knew of them, they were right. Amendment V was more a research and publicity organization than one made up of practicing criminal lawyers. Although they were great at filing motions and arguing appeals, when it came time to do the heavy lifting of an actual criminal trial, their resources would be a bit strained.

"Bernie stepped up," I muttered, wondering how much of it was public zeal and how much guilt over not having helped out before.

Her eyes drew together in puzzlement. "Were you really a wrestler?"

"Sure."

"For how long?"

I wasn't sure exactly what that had to do with anything, but figured talking to me was better than her scowling at me. "A good chunk of years, up until I was pushing forty."

"You any good?"

I gave her one of the Blond Bomber's patented smiles. "I made a living."

"You win much?"

I narrowed my eyes. Sitting in front of her, Sheila didn't seem like the sharpest blade in the woodshed, though she didn't seem all that slow either. Was it possible she was the last living person on earth who didn't know pro wrestling was, as they like to say nowadays, scripted?

Then I remembered she'd been stuck away in prison for decades and had her whole life ripped from her. She'd had more important things to occupy her mind.

"I did okay," I said. "Let's get back to you. When Bernie first saw you, did he say anything about money?"

"You know, I don't even know for sure. I was kind of in a daze."

"Being arrested will do that to you," I said.

"Yeah. I do remember him saying not to worry about anything, that one way or the other he'd get me out. Look around you. Does it look like I'm out?"

"I know it's hard to think like this, Sheila, but it hasn't been that long. Trust me, he's working on it. Before I go any further, there's something I need to know. Two things, actually."

She looked at me for a moment, her eyes hooded over, then shrugged. "Then ask."

"Did Bernie ask you if you killed Robert Harris? Did he want to know one way or the other?"

"No, he didn't seem concerned about that."

"Did you?"

"Did I what?"

"Kill Harris," I said, struggling not to throw up my hands in frustration.

She stared down at the table rather than at me. Not a good sign.

She mumbled something I didn't quite catch.

"Come again?" I asked.

"Bastard took my life from me. All those bastards did."

"Sheila," I began, worried that, Constitution be damned, someone was listening in.

"Whole goddamned fuckin' corrupt system took it all from me. I didn't have a chance from the start. They had it all stacked."

"Mrs. Hampton," I tried again.

She raised her eyes, and if I hadn't have been such a tough guy I would have run screaming from the room.

The balefulness in her gaze could have cut diamonds.

"No, goddamnit. I didn't kill anyone. Ever. I'll tell you, though. Right about now I sure wish I would have."

CHAPTER TWELVE

I RECEIVED A TEXT FROM BERNIE as I was climbing into the Cherokee. I obviously had some questions for him, but figured then wasn't the time to go into it. I read the text over, then opened up a separate file he'd sent. After I took my time reading that, I fired up the car and headed out. He'd managed to come up with a lead for me to follow. Maybe not much of one, but any port in a storm.

About twenty minutes later I pulled to the curb next to a single-story tract house on the far west side of town. It wasn't all that long ago that this area of Providence had been undeveloped land, rolling hills that stretched to the horizon. Then, about ten years ago, the town started growing, and it was a lot easier to develop around those small hills then deal with some of the more forested areas to the south and north.

The hills were still there, and they seemed to go on forever, as they always had, though in order to appreciate them you had to look past all the homes and small shopping strips that had popped up.

I grew up in this area, and I could remember the shock I felt a little over five years ago, when I'd left St. Louis and the wrestling life behind, returning home to Providence to settle into my two new careers: running a gym and professional snooping on the side. The amount of forested, wild area that had been turned over to development had been a bit of a heart stopper.

I stepped out of the car and looked over the house and yard. Well maintained, no peeling paint, hardly any weeds to be found. An open garage to the right revealed an array of shiny yard and carpentry tools, along with an old Harley Davidson that appeared to be about halfway through a restoration project.

From somewhere in the neighborhood came the whine of a power saw.

Stepping up on the porch, I rang the bell twice before someone yelled from around the house.

"Back here."

Following a cobbled path, I went around the west side of the house and unlatched a redwood gate. The cobbles continued into the backyard, eventually ending next to a mid-sized patio arrayed with wrought iron furniture.

A man in his mid-fifties, with a full head of salt and pepper hair and the slightest hint of a pot belly, stood in front of two saw-horses, measuring a couple of pine boards stretched across.

"Mike Palmer?" I asked, even though I recognized him.

Palmer glanced up from his measuring, a pair of the brightest blue eyes I'd ever seen boring into me. When I'd seen his name on the file Bernie had sent, I remembered him mainly because of those eyes.

"You're not a salesman," he said. "Not dressed like that. Or with hair like that."

"Come on, Mike. You know me."

Palmer dropped the tape measure and stood all the way up.

"Of course I do, Quinton. It hasn't been that long. What are you doing here?"

I paused, wondering if he actually didn't know. Palmer had spent his whole life as a uniformed police officer, up to a few years back when he'd pulled the pin and retired. We weren't friends, really. As far as that goes, not even much in the way of acquaintances.

We'd bumped into each other a couple of times since I'd returned to town, usually at parties, bars or card games. And while he'd never been in my gym, at least as far as I remembered, he'd obviously been doing something to keep himself in shape.

Palmer had been one of those die-hard cops, the sort who start in uniform and end their career, decades later, still in uniform. He'd never even been moved up to sergeant, though according to Bernie he'd been offered promotion more than once. Each time, he'd elected to stay on the streets rather than sit behind any sort of a desk.

In his time, Palmer had been involved, at least on the street level, with some major events in Providence, including the murder of Derek Hampton. The senior officer in the first car arriving on the scene, he'd conducted the initial interview of Sheila Hampton, and certain notations he'd made and questions he'd asked had pointed the detectives, when they arrived on the scene, in her direction.

Although they would have gotten there fairly quickly in any case because the person closest to the deceased, especially the spouse, is always the primary suspect. Even so, Palmer had started the ball rolling.

Now here he stood asking me what I wanted.

"You hear any news today, Mike?" I asked.

"Naw. Since I put in my papers I hardly pay any attention to what's going on. Just leave me alone to work around the house and I'm fine."

"Not even local news?"

He grinned. "Especially not local news. What's up, Quinton? What can I do for you?"

"Surely you heard Sheila Hampton was released from prison last week."

Palmer reached over to a small table and picked up a pack of cigarettes. Tamping one out, he got it going with a lighter lying next to the pack.

Yep, the guy was old school all the way.

"'Course I heard about that. Only had about a hundred reporters around the country calling me to get my reaction. I told all of them the same thing I'll tell you. What the hell do I care? She was a footnote in an incident report more than twenty years ago. And if she turned out innocent, what the hell? I'm not the one who made the call to arrest her."

His hands were trembling a bit. I wondered if he'd decided to fire up a smoke to cover up his nervousness.

I couldn't quite make the guy out. I could understand working a job long enough that when you quit you didn't want to keep in touch with it at all. Sure, I could get that. But I couldn't quite imagine no one had called him at some point this morning, if for no other reason than to mention the weird coincidence.

"Had you heard she's been arrested again?" I asked.

He peered at me, puzzlement on his face. If he was acting, he was doing one hell of a job.

"Hadn't heard. But I'm not surprised."

"Why's that?"

"'Cause she's a criminal. Once a crook always a crook."

"She was let out and given a new trial," I said.

He took a puff and blew the smoke in my direction. I didn't bother stepping out of the way. In my wrestling days I spent enough time in smoke-filled locker rooms, small arenas and night clubs that it didn't bother me.

"Cleared or not, the woman's a murderer. Why don't you get to it, Quinton? Why are you out here bothering me? I've work to do."

"They're saying she killed Robert Harris."

That one registered. Palmer blanched, and a small tic started under his left eye.

"You don't say?"

"Yup," I said. "Out of prison barely a week, new chance to set her record straight, and she guns down the prosecutor who put her away."

I left it at that for a moment, waiting to see if he had any sort of comeback. He'd managed to recover his composure as he took another drag on his smoke.

"That's wild," he finally said, "although I don't see why you're bothering me about it."

"It's like this." I wished he'd invite me inside, or at least to sit down. "Her lawyer and I are looking at the possibility that she was set up, at least for this Harris thing, and I was hoping you could possibly point me in the direction of someone who'd be out to get her."

He ground the cigarette out in a crystal ashtray resting on

the wrought iron table in front of him. The twitch under his eye had returned.

"Let me say this once Quinton, before you get the hell off my property, and make myself clear. I was a patrol cop the entire time I was on the force, nearly thirty damned years. I stayed on the streets all that time, lost count of the number of times I refused promotion. And I did it for only one reason."

He paused to give me time to ask the reason, though I had the distinct impression he didn't care if I asked or not. When I kept quiet, he continued.

"And that one reason was that I didn't want anything to do with politics, whether departmental, local or whatever. I didn't want to take sides or do anything outside the official scope of my duties. Never had a wife, don't have any kids, didn't need all that much money to live on, either then or now that I'm retired. In other words, I don't have any idea who would want to shanghai Sheila Hampton. I only met her the once, when my unit answered the call about her husband's death. Talked to the lady for a few minutes, then turned her over to the suits when they showed up. The only other time I saw her was a few months later when I got called to testify at her trial, and then she and I didn't so much as exchange a look. You got it?

"I do," I said.

"Other than that, I had nothing to do with her case. Don't come around again asking me about dead prosecutors or crooked judges or anything like that. I'm retired and I'm going to stay that way, both in body and spirit. Okay?"

His voice hadn't gotten any louder, but his tone sure had toughened up there at the end, his voice almost rasping. We stared each other down for a second or two, two men who had lived rather hard lives, both of us past our prime (though he had about a decade on me) before I decided to back down.

"Okay," I said as I turned and headed to his gate.

I could feel him watching even as I passed into the front yard and climbed into my car. Firing up the engine, I headed out, feeling his eyes boring into the back of my head.

I'd come to the guy for information, some little thread that could point me in the right direction, and I'd lucked out. In blowing me off, he'd given me a direction to go, whether intentional or not I had no idea yet.

Crooked judges?

CHAPTER THIRTEEN

Lois T. Jackson had been the presiding judge on Sheila's first trial. At the time, Jackson had served on the superior court of Carson County for a little over a decade. A whiz kid who'd made it through law school by the age of twenty-one. She'd been elected at a fairly young age, after only a few years' experience on both the prosecutorial and defense sides of the legal equation, with the result that the day before Sheila Hampton stood accused before her court Judge Jackson had celebrated her forty-fifth birthday.

At the time, I'd been living in St. Louis and just beginning to work for the Midwest Wrestling League. I hadn't yet actually performed in a show or anything. Instead, the owner had me working more as a roustabout on the shows: setting up the ring, tearing it down afterwards, taking tickets and being pretty much an all-around gopher.

With my hometown only a little over a hundred miles to the west, I was vaguely aware of the trial at the time, most of the media in Missouri covered it to one extent or another. It wasn't on my radar all that much. I was too busy splitting my time between trying to become a wrestling star, roaming the bar and club circuit with the guys to score as many babes as we could, and pursuing, in the most gentlemanly ways possible, the woman who would eventually become my ex-wife.

The noteworthy thing for me, where Lois Jackson was

concerned, was at an age where most jurists were thinking of hanging it up and retiring to the teaching and lecture life, she was hanging in there.

I'd gotten most of this from the file Bernie had sent me. Something didn't quite sit right. I called him at his office.

"Let me get this straight," I said. "She's some sort of whiz kid, makes it through law school while most people her age are learning how to balance a checkbook. She works both sides of the street long enough to pad her resume, runs for judge and wins. All of this before she's thirty-five and just stays in the same slot for the rest of her career?"

"Most people don't use checkbooks anymore, Sam."

"I know that Bern. My point is—"

"I get your point, and you're right. It does look odd."

"She have close roots here?"

"Not anymore. Her kids are grown, husband passed away about five years back, no grandkids that I know of."

"Hold on there. Her husband died five years ago? If he was anywhere near her age, that would put him in his fifties or sixties."

"Phillip Jackson was sixty-five at the time of his death. I attended the funeral. Along with most of the central Missouri legal profession."

"He a judge too?"

"Lawyer. One of the best in civil litigation. What's it matter?"

"Just trying to put everything together, Bern. She's lived around here all of her adult life and doesn't see any reason to move. Okay. But there are surely higher-level things she can be doing without leaving the area. What about politics or the state courts? The capital's just down the road."

Bernie hemmed and hawed for a couple of minutes.

"You thinking there's something a bit off about her situation?" he asked.

"How'd she react to Sheila's verdict being overturned?"

"Far as I know, she didn't make any kind of public comment. But I have to tell you, I think you're off base here. I've worked around the woman for decades now, been in front of her in court I can't tell you how many times. If someone is putting the screws to Sheila, Lois is the last person who'd be involved."

Although I had respect for Bernie's opinion, and he clearly knew the local judicial scene better than I did, I wasn't ready to write anyone off just yet.

"What about the other principals in the case?" I asked.

"What about them?"

"Can you get me the rundown on each of them?"

Bernie didn't reply. I pulled up to a red light while he stayed silent and sat through and proceeded on the green before he answered.

"Sam," he said, "you realize that if you start turning over rocks, who knows what kind of vermin will crawl out."

"Isn't that why you hired me, Bernie?"

"It is. I just want to make sure that you're clear on how bad this can get."

"Fair enough. And while we're at it, who hired you?"

"Huh?"

"I went back to see Sheila."

"You shouldn't have done that without me, Sam. She's my client and . . ."

"I thought she was our client, Bernie. As long as we're arguing semantics, why didn't you tell me that you went to her, instead of her coming to you?"

"I don't see how that's germane to . . ."

"Come on, Bern. Ever since this morning you've been walking around like there's some deep, dark secret you want to get out. What's the big issue here?"

There was a long pause, followed by Bernie's voice filled with what, on anyone else, would sound like regret.

"Not yet, Sam. Please. I've got to work out whatever it is on my own. Okay?"

My shoulders slumped. "Okay Bern, for now. Get that info together and e-mail it to me. I'm going to swing by the gym for a few things. Alright?"

We both said our goodbyes. The Blaster was just a few blocks

away now. I had the feeling, growing stronger by the minute, that
I'd taken this thing a bit too lightly when Bernie walked through
my door that morning.

CHAPTER FOURTEEN

O RDINARILY, I'D SAY THE NEXT STEP called for caution.
Confronting a sitting judge, let alone more or less implying
she may have been involved in throwing a major trial, is something
most folks should think long and hard about doing.

When the potential confronter was in possession of a professional license, and a mere word or two in the right ear from said
judge could result in the aforementioned license being discarded
like a Burger King bag on the shoulder of the highway, one should
seriously consider such a blatantly stupid action.

Ordinarily, that's what I'd say. But I'd already been given a push
in the right direction by Mike Palmer.

And since I had no clue who else was talking to whom, I figured
I'd better strike before anyone got together on their story.

Provided there was a story to get together on.

I wasn't yet all in with Bernie's view of the case. I thought it
entirely likely that Sheila had killed her husband. It would fit the
oldest pattern in the world. But a guilty woman being unexpectedly set free? Would she have reason to commit an obvious crime
that would land her right back in prison, especially when any third
grader would see her as the obvious suspect?

Far as that went, if Sheila hadn't been around as such a convenient suspect, who would have been next in line? Who would have
had it in for Derek Hampton?

The way I looked at it, whether Sheila had killed Derek or not, it was quite a stretch to believe she'd done in Robert Harris.

I was planning on talking to Judge Jackson at her home, the address kindly supplied by my lawyer friend Bernie Lyman, rather than at her place of work. Much more legal jeopardy for me doing it that way, though I figured if I managed to catch her with her guard down, and no one around to help her out, I'd get some truth out of her.

Provided, again, that there was any truth to be had.

It had been a long, kind of furious day, and the sun was beginning to dip downwards a bit before I realized I hadn't had anything to eat since breakfast. I turned my Cherokee to the west, and a few minutes later was plopped in a booth in my favorite burger place, just off Arena Avenue, eagerly awaiting a double cheeseburger with everything and basket of fries. My little red-headed waitress had already brought me a mug of beer, and all I wanted to make my day complete was my food.

What happened instead was that a man of early middle age, vaguely Hispanic in appearance, wearing a light gray suit slid into the other side of my booth. He wasn't all that big, but he wasn't exactly a lightweight either. A couple of inches under six feet, slender with obvious lean muscle under the tailored suit, he had a thatch of brown hair and dark brown eyes that, at the moment, were boring into me.

If I wasn't the rough-and-tumble type of guy I am, I may have been a little intimidated.

The suit did not match with "cop." It looked to be all silk, and the tone-on-tone shirt underneath had French cuffs, with small gold cuff links attached. The tie, a pale red with gray and blue paisleys, no doubt cost as much as my entire outfit.

I took a long chug of beer, just to show I wasn't intimidated. Or maybe so he wouldn't see my hands shaking.

Even sitting silently, the dude exuded a cold, cold air.

"The other tables full?" I asked.

"I figured it was time we were acquainted," he said.

"Me too," I answered.

He blinked at that one. "You know who I am?"

"No, but about the time you sat down I figured we should get to know each other."

The man leaned back in the booth and undid the button on his jacket. "Yeah, that's what Nichols and the others said. That you tend to speak before you think."

The mention of Josh Nichols pinged something in my brain. Before I could respond, the little redhead came by and deposited my food in front of me. She glanced at my companion, who shook his head, and asked if I wanted anything else. I replied in the negative, and she smiled and went away.

The two patties of my burger were hanging over the edges of the bun, dripping grease into the basket, while three different kinds of cheese practically bubbled at me. My stomach growled, but I didn't want the man in front of me to think me a pig as his first impression. Plus, he'd given me that hint to follow up.

"You're Lieutenant Santiago, right?" I asked.

He stretched his hand across the table, being sure not to dip his jacket sleeve into my burger basket. "William," he said.

"Good to know you, Bill," I said as I withdrew my hand.

"William," the cop emphasized.

I looked away and began digging into my burger. "What can I do for you?" I asked after a couple of bites.

"Like I said, I figured it was about time. I'm new in town and been getting caught up on all the ins and outs."

I hesitated at that one, my burger half raised to my mouth. "Which am I?"

"Well, that's the thing," the cop said. "I'm working that out. Nichols and a couple of the other guys speak rather highly of you."

I gave him a grin.

"Conversely, some of the brass and city leaders describe you as a real pain in the ass."

"Can't please all the people all the time," I said.

Santiago stared at me, and I took another bite of my burger. It was almost gone, and I hadn't enjoyed it yet.

"Maybe not," he continued. "But I read up on the role you played in the whole O'Brien mess earlier in the year."

"How'd I come out?" as I snagged a couple of French Fries with my fingers.

Santiago raised his hand up, held horizontally, and wagged it back and forth.

"Not bad," I said. "Wanna start a fan club?"

The horizontal hand, held in mid-air, slammed straight down on the table, smacking loud enough that most of the nearby diners turned and stared at us.

Over behind the cash register, one of the clan of brothers who owned the place, a big, beefy guy of Italian ancestry, glanced our way. I waved at him, and he nodded and went back to figuring receipts.

"And now," Santiago said, "I find you messing around in the Harris homicide."

"Uh huh," I said, working to impress him with my wit.

"Uh huh. And I don't think I approve."

Most righteous citizens would quail before the display of angered authority. Then again, most righteous citizens didn't have Bernie Lyman in their corner.

Plus, during my ring days I'd been hit over the head and back a lot with steel chairs, which develops a certain toughness of the spirit.

"It's not for you to approve or disapprove," I said. "I've been employed by Mrs. Hampton's attorney to perform certain investigations. If you've a problem with that, take it up with the state licensing board."

Santiago leaned back, a slight smile on his face. "I'd heard you don't back down too easily, Quinton. I'm wondering if you're as tough as you put out, though."

I popped a fry into my mouth. "I did help bust up a mob war, you know."

The cop's smile broadened. "I'm from Chicago, mister. What you call a mob war, we call a hectic Saturday night."

"Yeah, and you've been having a lot of hectic Saturday nights back there, haven't you? What'd they do? Send you down here to learn from real cops?"

The smile froze, and something glinted behind the lieutenant's eyes. The tendons in his hands tensed. He lifted himself up from his seat.

"You haven't done anything wrong yet, Quinton, and you should be damned careful that you don't. You mind one last piece of advice?"

"Why not," I said.

"Uh huh. Here it is then, private. You may know everyone in this area, and they may all think you're the cat's balls, but fuck with me and you'll barely live to regret it. Okay?"

I thought about nodding my understanding. I stared back for a few heartbeats till he must have thought I'd gotten the message and turned to walk off.

As he left the restaurant, I thought of sending Josh Nichols a sympathy card concerning his new boss. I wasn't sure he would appreciate the humor.

CHAPTER FIFTEEN

MY LITTLE ENCOUNTER WITH LT. SANTIAGO had me rethinking my plans. After meeting with Palmer, I'd intended going right up the chain, tracking down as many of the trial participants as I could and seeing what I could shake out of them about Sheila's conviction. While it was true that Bernie Lyman's primary concern had to be her current predicament, it felt obvious to me that it all somehow related back to her original conviction.

And I'd only begun flailing about with Officer Palmer when he threw out that line about judges.

Moving on from there, I had planned my next stop as the lead detective in Sheila's case, the one who'd been the main prosecution witness against her. Before I could make that move good ole' Lt. Santiago had interrupted my meal and set me in a new direction.

I figured my new, revised plan as a brilliant move.

Either that or just a foolhardy, dumbass stunt.

If you Googled "Hampton Industries," you'd end up with more pages than you could possibly read. Even if I narrowed it down to just "News" or "Finances," I'd have to hire four or five assistants to go through it all, sifting for any stray crumbs that could possibly be significant. I could have taken the easy route and just gone to their web site, which would only give me the polished, white-washed version of both the company and family. If I was after the straight dope, the unvarnished truth of the Hampton clan, why not go straight to the source?

I pulled my Cherokee up about two blocks down from the Hampton family home. It hadn't taken all that much effort to nail down that Derek's siblings, both still alive, lived in the family house. That may seem a little odd, considering their ages, but only if you weren't familiar with Providence society.

The Hampton "family home" occupied something like four or five acres on what had once been the far west side of town and was now merely the west side. Overall a fairly upscale neighborhood. Turning off of Broadway onto Kirkland St. and driving three blocks south, it didn't take long to spot the six-foot high yellow brick wall that stretched around approximately two and a half blocks of secluded residence.

Turning at the far south corner of the wall, it continued for another block before doubling back around. I circled the entire estate twice before spotting, midway down the east stretch, a small recessed driveway. There were no signs or scrollwork announcing the estate, no big double gates for entrance and exit. Merely a small little driveway with a plain gate and little pillbox for a guard.

Once I had it spotted, I circled around the whole area once more, pulling up to the curb a little ways down from the southeast corner. The house I parked in front of was nice, looked like it belonged to a stockbroker or banker, though probably nothing compared to whatever domicile squatted somewhere within that acreage just to the north.

I was using a standard process of elimination. Going on the assumption that Sheila hadn't murdered her husband, which I figured at, at best, fifty-fifty, it only made sense to look at who else would have benefited from Derek's Hampton's death. Once you took Sheila out of the equation, Derek's siblings became the next logical suspects.

Except that, as far as I knew, his other family members hadn't even been considered. As soon as the cops saw Sheila crouched in the corner with her hubby's body only a few feet away, they'd basically stopped looking. And when they'd found the gun that killed him with her prints on it, that was the whole game.

Actually, the setup sounded suspiciously like exactly what had gone down in the Harris killing. Maybe the notion of her complete innocence wasn't as farfetched as it sounded.

My phone beeped just as a dark blue Lincoln pulled up and parked about twenty feet in front of me. As I checked out the screen, a carbon copy of the first car pulled in the same distance behind me. Expecting the Hampton estate to have a slew of cameras and other security devices, I wasn't all that surprised at the reception.

Looking at the phone, I saw that Bernie had sent me what information he had on the appellate judges who had overturned Sheila's conviction and sentence. It looked like a sizable file, and I didn't want to take the time to check it out right then.

Drumming my fingers on the steering wheel, I contemplated my options as the doors on the Lincoln in front of me opened up and two men got out and came my way. They were corporate security drones all the way, down to the gray slacks, blue blazers and mirrored sunglasses they wore. At sundown, no less.

As the two approached my car, one on each side, I rolled down both front windows.

"Good evening, sir," the guy on my side, who looked to be mid-thirties, greeted me. He stood about five ten and had the corded, taut frame of a man who lifts weights for quality, not quantity. His black hair complemented a tan so dark as to almost be black itself, and his black eyes gave him a no-nonsense demeanor.

The guy leaned into my car, the blue blazer gaping open enough for me to glimpse a .45 in a shoulder holster on his left side. "Can I see some ID, please?"

"Why?" I asked, while giving him my "let's all be friends" smile that I'd practically patented during my time in the wrestling ring. The "let's all be friends" smile usually showed up right before I sucker punched some poor slob below the belt.

"Excuse me?" He gave me the slightest bit of a frown.

"Why do you want to see my ID?" I asked, keeping an eye on drone number two out of the corner of my eye. That guy looked about as disinterested as you could get about the whole thing. I wanted to check out if whoever was in the car behind me was up to anything but only had two eyes to handle the entire scene.

"Because you're acting suspiciously," my window buddy replied to my query.

"Really," I said. "What am I doing? Something nefarious like coming up to respectable citizens on the street and asking to see their ID?"

My new best friend frowned even more. I felt his pain. Keeping up the "let's all be friends" smile was becoming a strain.

"No, you're doing something suspicious, such as driving around the block a couple of times and then parking down from the estate over there." He jerked his thumb up the street to the Hampton place.

I took a minute to crane my head in a full 360. The guys behind me were just sitting there. With the windows darkened I couldn't even make out how many were in there, but I figured it for at least two.

"Looks like a public road to me," I said, turning back to the one standing outside my window. "Far as that goes, considering we're out in public, I doubt you have any authority to do anything to me."

"Maybe I don't need authority. Maybe my friends and I are tough enough to take care of a guy like you."

I shrugged, as I did surreptitiously grasping the door handle.

"Then again, maybe you're not," I said.

He paused for a minute, a slight tic developing in his right cheek. I assumed he was accustomed to bluffing people by looking and sounding important. With the Hampton money behind him, in most instances Mr. Important probably didn't have to do much more than bluff.

"I don't think you want to test us, fellow," he finally replied.

"Maybe, maybe not," I said. "But same goes for you."

"Huh?"

"Do you and your bros back there actually want to have a running battle in public? My guess is that the Hampton clan wouldn't care for publicity like that."

The guy leaned back from my door and waved his right hand in the direction of the car behind us. At the same time, the man over by my passenger door took a step back and moved his right hand partially towards the left side of his jacket.

Okay, maybe these guys did have expertise in something besides simple bluffing.

I started changing my plans as well. While I kept my left hand on the door handle, I began easing my right towards the ignition. I'd only made it a few inches, though, when my doorman spoke up.

"If I were you, Mr. Quinton, I'd refrain from starting my car."

I jerked a bit at that. Not much, just enough that a pair of sharp eyes could have seen it. I wondered how the hell he'd learned my name in just the few minutes we'd been talking and took a closer look.

Sure enough, he was wearing some sort of earbud, one so light colored and recessed I hadn't caught it at first. I figured the men in the rear car had checked out my license plate and run it through the system to get my name. DMV records are supposed to be sealed to all except law enforcement, but we all know how much that counts in the modern era.

Plus, the speed with which they'd managed it caused a little roll in my belly. I doubted if even the police chief could have gotten a readout that quickly.

"You sound pretty sure of yourself," I said. "What are you going to do if I drive away? Chase me down and sideswipe me?"

My friend shook his head, a sort of half smirk on his face.

"We wouldn't have to do anything that drastic, bub. We've enough clout with people who matter that we could have your PI license stripped before you could blink."

I felt a slow burn beginning in my gut and did my best to tamp it down.

"What are we gonna do? Sit out here yakking at each other until we both faint from hunger?" I asked.

Another sort of smirk as the guy briefly held his hand up to his ear. I waited, working to keep my breathing steady.

A second later, he took his ear down and his smirk turned to an actual smile.

"Actually, we don't have to do anything like that," he said. "If you're amenable, Mr. Quinton, my employers would like to speak with you."

CHAPTER SIXTEEN

LIKE MOST PROVIDENCE RESIDENTS, I'd always wondered what lay inside the gates of the Hampton estate. Carson county isn't exactly known for families of vast wealth, but that's only because they keep themselves fairly well hidden. Over the five years that I'd worked in the area as a PI, I'd bumped into more than one person who could buy and sell me all day long without even noticing it. And one or two of my gym clients had bank accounts with more zeroes than most people could count.

Offhand, the average citizen could name six or seven major, international companies whose owners or founders lived within our city limits. While we have something of a reputation of a sleepy college town, the truth is Providence and the surrounding area probably hold, per capita, the same amount of wealth as St. Louis, Chicago or New York.

I'd driven my own car into the place, with my new buddy from the street riding shotgun. The two cars flanked us as the gates swung open and we went past the little security pillbox. I thought about waving to the uniformed guard manning the gate, then figured that there was a camera clocking my every move, and someone would see it as bad form and report me to Lieutenant Santiago.

How many people called on the owners of the Hampton manse wearing jeans and a tee shirt?

Past the gate, the driveway went straight for about fifty feet before turning to the right and following a meandering course through the grounds. We passed a couple of out buildings, part of a golf course (looked like nine holes all told), and a few more security stations, plus a whole lot of trees. The whole thing, considering the size of the grounds, reeked of sedate understatement.

I'd almost expected there to be two or three mansions somewhere within those grounds, and possibly there were, but when we pulled up to the main house, or at least what I assumed was the main one, I noticed again how simple the architecture was.

Three stories tall, with a decent spread, a long, winding porch that wrapped around to the sides and held several chairs and tables. Plain white in color, the windows in front large but not all that over the top, and the flowers and shrubbery all around well-cared for although, once again, not all that extravagant.

Okay, point taken. The Hamptons had enough wealth that they didn't need to show it off. Maybe they'd be wearing jeans and tee-shirts as well.

I had a sneaking suspicion that somewhere behind the main digs there'd be a bungalow bachelor pad with all sorts of motor-cycles, luxury cars and ATV's lying around.

I stopped where my passenger told me to, and the two of us got out, our front and rear escorts pulling up about forty feet away on each side. It looked as if the head honcho, who hadn't yet introduced himself, was going to take me in alone, which was either overly risky or scornful of my abilities. Not sure which, I decided to test it out.

I turned as we reached the top of the front porch steps.

"You going to take me right in without frisking me first?" I asked.

Security Dude almost snickered at that one.

"You aren't packing, Quinton. Any rookie cop could see that."

Okay, so much for that.

He didn't knock, just opened the door and strode right in, and I followed behind him. I glanced around as casually as possible and couldn't see any cameras on us as we entered a spacious foyer, but I had to assume they were there.

"Follow me," my escort said. "And don't get cute."

"Me?" I asked, wearing the most innocent face I could. "I've never been cute in my life."

"I can believe it," he said, his face as flat as a mask. "When I was a kid, I used to see you wrestle."

"Didn't know you were a fan," I said.

"I'm not. My friends and I were usually rooting for the other guy," he chuckled.

Alright, he had a sense of humor.

A few seconds later we entered a small sitting room, complete with dark brown leather furniture and oak desk. My escort didn't sit, instead merely stood in the middle of the room. I figured, what the hell, and sat down in one of the rich leather easy chairs. My companion frowned at me.

A moment later a door on the side of the room opposite that which we entered opened up, and two people, a man and a woman, walked in. They looked to be somewhere in their fifties, though rich people have access to enough resources, whether medical, nutritional or herbal, that they could have been well preserved sixties.

Both medium height, the man a little pudgy and the woman looking in good condition, as if she played three or four sets of tennis a week. They both had brown hair and eyes. The man's hair was almost entirely dark, kind of weirdly offset by a pair of bushy white eyebrows, which inclined my estimate of his age to early sixties or so. The woman also had dark hair, though hers was far along the way to turning silver.

I glanced at them before deliberately settling into my chair a little more.

"Thanks, Marcus. You can leave us now," the woman said.

"You sure, ma'am? I'm glad to stay in case you need. . ."

"Not necessary. My brother and I can handle this."

She had a definite bite in her voice, almost as if she spent time daily practicing the most demeaning way to order people around.

I glanced at the security man as he turned to leave the room.

"Marcus?" I said, putting a bit of a lilt into my voice.

The guy was good. He didn't miss a step as he naturally swerved a foot in my direction. "Be careful where you step, old man," he said as he left the room.

"I'm George Hampton," the older man introduced himself as he did a half turn to the woman flanking him, "and this is my sister Mary."

Yeah, definitely well preserved. If they'd been Derek's older siblings at the time of the first trial, they were surely well into their sixth decades.

I didn't say anything, as they obviously knew who I was.

"Can we get you anything to drink before we get down to business, Quinton?"

"I'm fine," I said. "Just waiting to hear what you want so I can leave and get on with my life."

The two of them sat, Mary wearing a severe frown and George smiling at me.

"Believe me, Mr. Quinton." At least he was more polite than his sister. "We want you to get on with things, just as long as whatever you do doesn't involve us."

"Why should it?" I asked. "I don't even know why you had Gonzo out there pull me in here."

Shaking his head, George stood up and walked over to a small sideboard and fixed himself a shot of bourbon. He glanced at his sister, who shook her head.

"Do us a favor, Quinton," Mary said as her brother came back over and sat down across from me. "Don't treat us like idiots, okay? We're not the sort of lowlifes you're used to dealing with."

"Lowlifes?" I did my best to arch one eyebrow, like Spock used to do in *Star Trek*, but didn't quite pull it off.

"We've checked you out," Mary responded, "and we've learned all about your—tenuous—businesses. We're willing to deal with you respectfully if you'll accord the same to us."

Her tone sounded respectful but came across as a cobra eyeing a rabbit.

"Okay," I said, figuring the fewer syllables I used around these two the better off I'd be.

"We only have one question," Mary said. "Why are you bothering to work for the woman who murdered our brother?"

Several witty replies came to mind.

For once, I managed to tamp them all down.

"From what I understand, that was just deemed a wrongful conviction," I said.

George frowned at me.

"She was released," he said, finally getting into the conversation, "which doesn't mean she was innocent. Only that the first trial had its flaws."

"George," I said. "I think you need to refresh a little bit on how our legal system works."

His white eyebrows narrowed, almost forming a unibrow, and a faint flush appeared around his neck. Mary reached over to place a restraining hand on his leg.

"What my brother means is that, despite the appellate court's decision, we believe her to be guilty."

Not knowing how to respond to that, I stayed quiet.

"And," she continued, "the fact that she's already been rearrested would seem to validate our beliefs. No matter how many breaks you give someone, trash will out."

"If you say so." Four syllables, maybe I should rein it in a bit.

"Why are you working for that woman?" George sounded almost conciliatory. I wondered which of them ran the company board meetings.

"I'm not," I said. "I'm working for her attorney."

Attaboy Sam, fluster them with doubletalk.

"And that gives you license to snoop around our property like some common thug?" George snapped.

I was getting a little tired of this. "Mr. Hampton, I was driving on a public street. I never set foot on your grounds, nor did I intend to. When your goons dropped in on me, I was parked on said public street. Had been there for all of five minutes. I didn't have any sort of camera, lenses or anything along that line. If you think you've got something on me, call the cops and press some made-up charges. Wouldn't be the first time, right?"

Although that last quip had been pretty much a shot in the dark, it caused Mary's posture to tighten up enough I was afraid her spine would snap.

Okay, I may have just learned more than I had all day long on this case.

"I doubt that will be necessary, Mr. Quinton," George said. "And I think you're slightly confused about us. Our only desire through any of this is to make sure that our brother's killer is held to account for her actions."

"You held her to account for going on a quarter century," I pointed out. "What happened?"

Now it was Mary's turn to flush, though she held it together a lot better than her brother, who was rapidly hyperventilating beside her. I figured I'd better get out of there before I found myself guilty of involuntary manslaughter.

No doubt Mary agreed with me.

"I think you'd better leave now. My brother and I only wanted to meet you and see what it is you wanted. We had no idea you'd turn out to be such a . . . a . . ."

"Sweetheart?" I supplied.

"Laborer," she supplied back to me.

"I'd rather be called a thug, but to each his own."

"Goodbye, Mr. Quinton. I'm sure you can find the way out, and Marcus will take you back to your car."

CHAPTER SEVENTEEN

MARCUS WAS WAITING FOR ME on the porch outside.
"Ready to go, slick?" he asked as I approached. I stared at him for a minute.

He struck me as the kind of competent tough that could fool a person. Put him in the right setting, and he'd look like a salesman. Change the clothes and a few other things and he'd fit right in in a poolhall.

And even though I outweighed the guy by about fifty pounds or more, I wasn't too confident which of us would win if we mixed it up.

"Sure," I said. "Let's head out."

We got into my car without another word and began the winding, convoluted drive back to the street. He didn't say anything until we approached the gates and waited for the pillbox guy to raise the barrier.

"You should steer clear of them," he said while staring straight out the windshield.

I glanced his way for the absolute briefest moment, then mimicked his staring routine. As the gates opened up, I goosed the accelerator the slightest bit and we headed out the drive.

I waited, assuming there would be another word or two of wisdom coming.

"You're a tough guy," Marcus said as we swept out of the driveway and onto the street. He glanced my way. "Yeah, we checked you out. You have a solid rep around the local cops, and you were involved in that mob business a few months back."

"You mustn't have checked very close," I said. "These days, most of the cops in town would prefer I fall off the edge of the earth."

I pulled up behind the two security cars and shifted into park. Marcus angled himself in the seat to face me.

"Don't be too sure, Quinton. You may have more support among the force than you think you do."

I stared at the man for a minute, tumblers clicking into place in my head.

"I'll take your word for it, but I'm awfully curious right about now. You tracked all that down in the half an hour since I pulled up here?"

Marcus grinned, which made him look something like a shark. "You're dealing with a different type of people here, Quinton. The shady promoters you used to wrestle for, the two-bit syndicate guys you took down a while back, they're nothing compared to the Hamptons. Giving you a fair warning here. You fuck around with them, and you'll just disappear. Won't even be a trace left that you ever existed left."

Although understanding his point, I took points off for exaggeration.

"Back to my question," I said. "How'd you dig up all that info so fast?"

"That's what I'm trying to tell you, Blond Bomber. It wasn't that fast. We've been onto you since this morning, since before you even knew about this case."

My gut began feeling cold. I worked to keep a light-hearted look on my face. "Lyman," I said.

My new buddy and confidante smiled. "They've had us watching Lyman since he and Sheila first hooked up. How's that for reach?"

I shook my head, trying to wrap my mind around what he'd just said. It even went deeper than them watching Bernie and seeing him come to me.

"How'd they know?" I asked, my gut clenching at the possible answer.

The Hamptons' muscle man gave me that shark's smile again, if anything even wider than before.

"Wouldn't you like to know. See what I mean about reach, Quinton? And trust me on this. With those two, it's more than business. Sometimes I think they actually get their rocks off by fucking with people's lives. Now do yourself a favor, buddy, and get the hell out of here. And don't come back around."

I stared at him for a moment, thinking about starting something up. I figured that wouldn't accomplish much of anything, and besides, two grown men scuffling in a car would look kind of silly to anyone who happened to pass by. And I figured I had to keep my reputation, such as it was, as intact as possible.

For once in my life, I did the sensible thing and watched as he exited the Cherokee and joined up with his buddies.

I mentally reserved the right to come back if I wanted to.

CHAPTER EIGHTEEN

I DROVE ABOUT A MILE OR TWO away from the estate, then turned into the parking lot of a Rite-Aid, pulled out my phone and called Bernie.

It felt like I was spending all my time either calling or talking to Bernie.

He picked up on the second ring, and I could hear a couple of young voices, one male and one female, arguing in the background.

"What's up?" Bernie asked.

"I just met George and Mary Hampton." The arguing behind me got a little louder, but not enough for me to make out what they were saying.

"Are they a sweet couple of folks or what?" Bernie asked.

"You know them?"

"Not too well. Never worked for or against them. Met up a couple of times at various charity and social things. What'd they want?"

"I think mainly to tell me to lay off. What the hell's going on behind you?"

Bernie chuckled. "A couple of my associates, under the assumption that they are in charge of trial strategy, having a slight disagreement. It'll work itself out."

"Not for Sheila's case?"

"Of course not. You think I run a successful firm on one client at a time?"

"What I called about . . ." I began before Bernie interrupted.

"Would you two take it somewhere else?" he shouted away from the phone. "And while you're at it remember who signs the checks around here."

An instant later I heard a door shut.

"Okay," he came back on, his voice a lot more subdued. "What's the latest?"

While Bernie had been haranguing his associates, I'd scoped out the area around the parking lot. Everything looked normal as far as I could see. In a minute, I was going to have to step outside and check my Cherokee over.

"As I was saying, Bern, I just came from scoping out the Hampton estate. While doing so, I was approached by their security people and escorted inside."

"While doing so? You know, Blondie, you're talking less and less like a rassler every day."

"You think I'm starting to grow up?"

Bernie snorted. "Maybe. But I'm not holding my breath. You fumbled the play and their guards took you in for a pow wow. And?"

Although I gritted my teeth at the phrase "fumbled the play," I didn't rise to the bait. Bernie's one of those guys you either have to take as is or leave, and sometime back I'd decided to take him as he was.

"The point is," I said, in as calm as voice as possible, "that they knew who I was."

"Yeah? They probably checked out your plate and have someone inside the state government that could run it on the DQ."

"Exactly what they told me."

"Then what's the big deal, Sam? Why are you . . ."

"They knew I was working for you, Bern."

That one stopped him. I waited through a long pause, giving him time to digest it.

"Damn," he finally said.

"Yeah, pretty much my reaction."

Another stretched-out moment. If I'd closed my eyes, I could have seen the wheels turning in Bernie's head.

"Of course," he said after a minute or two, "it wasn't exactly a secret that I'd hired you."

"No."

"Quite a few people saw us down at the station today."

"There is that."

"And in court. Someone could have spotted you there."

"Also true," I said. "But the point is, Bern, why would anyone have cared enough to tell the Hamptons? For that matter, why would they have cared? What's in it for them?"

While the lawyer tussled with that one, I looked over the parking lot again. A scattering of early evening shoppers were coming and going, including one lady trying to lug a sack from the pharmacy, plus two squalling kids, to a faded red SUV. I didn't see anything I shouldn't have.

"Then the question is," Bernie eventually came back to me, "how did George and Mary know that I was working on this? Who clued them in?"

"That's one."

"And why they would even give a damn to bother with it?"

"If they think the woman who killed their brother is getting a free pass out of prison, I could see them being a tad bit interested."

Another of those extended silences as I let Bernie get to the destination I'd already arrived at.

Meanwhile, a black Corvette, complete with high-class rims and smoked windows, had swung into the parking lot from the west. It coasted to a stop, the engine running. I peered as hard as I could but couldn't make out any shapes or anything behind those darkened windows.

Surely something innocent, I thought. Guy doing shopping errands on his way home, stopping to call the little woman and see if she'd forgotten to put something on the list.

Could be a conscientious driver, too careful to answer his ringing phone while on the road. He pulls into the nearest parking lot and shifts into Park before answering.

Yeah, like that would happen in this town.

Woman from out of town perhaps, taking a minute to check the directions to her hotel.

Sure, could be any of those things.

Hired goons keeping tabs on a private eye who'd been nosing around the family manse?

The real killer of good old boy Robert Harris, scoping out someone who could queer his entire play?

And who the hell had smoked windows these days?

"Going with my working hypothesis," Bernie said.

"Yes?"

"The one that says Sheila was set up for killing Derek way back when."

"What any good defense attorney would claim," I said, implying that I had my doubts.

"The question is who would benefit from Derek's death."

"And the obvious answer is his heirs."

"Sheila was his main heir," Bernie pointed out.

"Come on, Bern. Even I know better than that. No one can profit from a crime they've been convicted of."

"Correct. But if for some reason Sheila couldn't have inherited . . ."

I wanted to smash my palm into my head at my denseness. "The estate would go to his nearest living relatives."

"More or less. There's always some litigation involved, but that's basically how it would work out."

"And since he and Sheila hadn't gotten around to popping out any baby Hamptons . . ."

"It would go to his siblings."

"And we're talking a lot of money, right?"

"Correct, and possibly even more than that."

"Oh?" I asked.

"Oh. Before their old man died, he installed Derek as the chairman of the company."

"The younger brother?"

"Kind of an unusual move, wouldn't you say?"

"Any idea how come?"

I could almost see Bernie shaking his head. "There's been gossip for years about it, but nothing I ever took too seriously."

"What kind of gossip?" I asked.

"You've got to keep in mind that Derek was quite a bit younger. Some talk has it that the old man thought of him as a golden child, could do no wrong type of kid."

"That usually tends to piss off the first born," I said.

The Corvette hadn't moved, nor had anyone exited it. I tossed out the "shopper on his way home" theory.

"Waitaminit, Bern," I said. "If her conviction was overturned last week, wouldn't that mean that she's entitled to his estate now?"

"And that's a headache for the civil lawyers. Common sense would say yes, though there's all sorts of issues that could intervene."

"You mean besides the fact that lawyers can find a way to bend any commonsense idea out of shape?" I asked.

"When this is all over," Bernie said, "remind me to be real pissed at you for that comment."

I grinned, at the same time deciding that it was time to catch the bull by the tail. Shifting into Drive, I crimped my wheel to the right.

"If she's innocent of Derek's killing," I asked, "but found guilty of Harris's, does that do anything to the estate split?"

"Again, common logic says no. Then again, who knows what some clever shyster could come up with."

"Shyster? And you say I bash your profession?"

I started inching the Cherokee in the direction of the Corvette, breathing a silent thanks that no other vehicles were close by. At the same time, I plunked my phone into one of those nifty holders on the console and reached down below my seat.

"Bern," I said, "call someone you know, who works fast and quiet, and get me a read on this license plate." I rattled off the number from the front plate of the Corvette.

"I'll give it my best shot Sam, but may need some time."

"Whatever, get it to me when you can."

"Something going on?" he asked.

"Catch you later, Bern," I said as I switched the phone off. By this point, I was about five feet in front of the Corvette's nose.

"Okay, bubba," I whispered to the Cherokee's interior, "let's play."

CHAPTER NINETEEN

THE CORVETTE'S OWNER obviously wasn't in a playful mood. With a roar of the engine and screech of the tires it shot backwards about twenty feet, then did a sharp right turn and headed out of the parking lot.

I did a quick 360 scan, saw not much in the way of possible collateral damage, and took off in pursuit.

It was a bit risky, for sure. Private eyes have to observe all the regular laws and rules as everyone else. The license in my wallet didn't come with any sort of official dispensation. Bounty hunters, those slugs, can pretty much violate any federal or state statutes they want and come out on top.

My profession, we're not that fortunate.

On the one hand I wanted to corner whoever was driving the 'Vette and get some answers from them, but I didn't want to snag the attention of any stray patrol cars ambling past. And I for sure didn't want to run down any innocent jaywalkers who happened to cross my path.

I figured, then, to tail the 'Vette for as long as I could, possibly trap them into some sort of box and, if necessary, bluff the hell out of them to get some information.

First, though, I had to keep them in sight. And as we headed down the road, more or less in the direction of Providence's western edge, one nagging question kept zipping around in my head like an errant pinball.

Who the hell does surveillance work in a black Corvette?

I spotted the car making a right on Vormster Street and kept going in a straight line. The next intersection up I did my own right, then powered through the next block as fast as I could. A cobalt blue Charger blared its horn at me as I almost scraped its passenger side.

I ignored the horn and kept on going. Another right on the second block, and about halfway to the next intersection I spotted my black 'Vette cruising along.

The sun had gone almost entirely down by now, and the night had assumed a kind of mixed-purple hue. The bright red lettering on a sign for our most ornate hotel, a downtown beacon, so to speak, was visible in the night sky, but clouds were keeping either stars or moon obscured, at least for the moment.

The 'Vette keeping to the speed limit told me that the driver, and passenger if there was one, figured they'd lost me. As they went down the street I kept on in my own direction, now heading at a right angle to them.

All this would have been a hell of a lot easier a month earlier, when the university students hadn't yet flocked into town, increasing Providence's population by a cool thirty percent. On the other hand, more traffic made it that much easier for a has-been, past his prime former wrestler to keep birddogging his quarry.

After a couple of blocks of zigging and zagging, I brought myself back on their street in their direction, keeping about half a block behind. By this point the sports car was clearly heading either out of town or to one of the housing communities that dotted the western edge of town, filled to bursting with homes whose property values brushed seven figures, though not quite as highly regarded as the Hampton neighborhood.

The 'Vette turned into a cul-de-sac off of a side street. Even with darkness coming on, I couldn't go in there without calling attention to myself. I pulled up to a curb about a hundred feet beyond, exited the Cherokee and paused to reconnoiter the neighborhood.

In the dark, it took me a minute to spot the 'Vette. Then I noticed it pulled in the drive of a two-story house, white with black trim and a slate-stoned walkway. The house had what looked like a two-car garage with the 'Vette parked in the driveway. Far as I could tell, the engine was turned off with the occupant, or occupants, nowhere to be seen.

I wanted a closer look at that house, but before I headed in, I pulled my phone out of my pocket and turned it off. Didn't want to be sneaking up on potential bad guys at the same time Bernie called me back with the license plate info or Lisa buzzed me wondering when I'd get back to the gym.

Before heading closer, I took about thirty seconds and listened as hard as I could. Because the homes in this subdivision are built a lot better than most modern construction, inside noises stayed inside. I saw a few lit windows here and there, plus the occasional flickering of a large-screen, plasma television. As hard as I looked and listened, I couldn't detect any sign of outside dogs.

Shrugging out of my jacket, I placed it on the passenger seat of the Cherokee, grabbed my gun from the console, locked my vehicle up, and headed out. I'd already plotted the circular route I would take to get to the house in question. What I would do once there wasn't as clear cut, but I figured making it up on the fly was better than taking my ball and running home.

There was a chance that the mystery car had nothing to do with the Sheila Hampton case, that someone unrelated to all of that had some, to them, legitimate reason for following me. But that was stretching coincidence a bit too far for my liking.

"Okay, Bomber," I whispered to the darkness, "time to go earn your money."

CHAPTER TWENTY

LOOKING AT ME, MOST PEOPLE ONLY SEE a big, slightly over-the-hill lug who appears about as graceful as a drunken bull. Folks don't much use the term "muscle bound" anymore, though anyone over fifty, who's ever read the back pages of a comic book, could easily imagine me walking down the beach, casually kicking sand in the face of some hapless nerd.

Goes to show what they know.

For several years, until I blew out one of my knees for the third and final time, I made my living as a pro wrestler. True, I only worked with the big boys for under a year, till the whole knee thing, but even though I spent most of my time in a small, local outfit, I managed to earn a living.

Well, more like scraped by a living.

When you wrestle in the indies, you do a lot more than perform in the ring. You have to sell tickets, set up the equipment, tear it all down and do any sort of gopher thing the boss needs done. All part of paying your dues.

I did all of that and more during those years.

It was in the ring where I excelled. And it doesn't matter how big or strong you are, you don't make it far in that business on brawn alone. There has to be quickness, agility and, in a lot of cases, stealth.

At least, stealth in terms of what the camera shows.

While I don't have a background in special forces or anything like that, I can move when I need to and a lot quicker and quieter than the average mope. This subdivision had some nice homes though it wasn't exactly a gated, patrolled community.

And for damned sure it wasn't a compound like the Hampton estate.

About five minutes later, as I scaled fences and avoided back porch lights and ducked under carports, I was in the backyard of the house in question.

'Course, these days you have to be on the lookout for those gadgets that send security vids to people's cell phones, and I came across three of those in the six houses I flitted past on the way to my target. Thankfully, no blaring alarms sounded behind me because I didn't want to leave any excuse for cops to come around later asking to check out the neighbors' security tapes.

If the residents of this neighborhood had dogs, they all must have been indoor pets.

When I stopped in the backyard of the house where the 'Vette had parked, I eased my way up to the porch, on the lookout for security gizmos and any stray Fidos that may be lurking around.

All clear.

From the porch, I eased my way alongside the house, rounding the southwest corner, looking in every window that I could.

Most of the windows had curtains drawn, and there were not that many. I could hear murmured sounds, some of which might have been voices, yet nothing distinct leapt out.

Halfway up the west side, it occurred to me that I was doing this the hard way. The easy way would be to go back to the Cherokee, drive away, find a quiet bar somewhere and wait for Bernie to get back to me with the info from the license plate. I could then make my move.

However, I was already here. Might as well find out whatever I could.

A few more steps had me alongside a side door that I assumed led into some kind of workroom or storage area. I stood there a moment, contemplating the possibility of sneaking in, when the mumbled sounds inside became louder, shriller.

Definitely voices now, and at least one of them becoming agitated.

The urge to get inside grew, and I reached out to try the knob on the side door. Locked, of course, but it felt old and wobbly. I almost thought I could turn it hard enough to snap the whole thing off.

Being caught breaking and entering wouldn't look all that hot the next time my PI license came up for renewal.

I waited.

A sharp noise, like a slap, came clearly through the wooden house side. Almost instantaneously, something tumbled over somewhere on the other side of the wall, and a woman screamed out.

I grabbed the cheap door lock and twisted it all the way to the side, managing to snap something in the interior shaft, so much for home security, and the door flew open.

I was standing in a small garage with another door on the other side. I crossed to the other door in about two seconds flat and found it unlocked.

I entered into the house's interior. I paused for a moment, listening as hard as I could, until I picked out more sounds of a struggle towards the rear. I moved to the doorway in the kitchen.

It contained a long breakfast bar running along one side, a middle island with an assortment of pots and pans hanging on bronze hooks from the ceiling, and a stove in one corner that had about twelve burners.

I saw the source of all the commotion.

And I recognized the identity of the mystery drive in the black 'Vette.

Karyn Roberts, the PR lady from KC and former crime reporter, was in the kitchen, struggling like hell with a brown-haired guy who looked as big and tall as me. Maybe a bit bigger, though his bulk tended more to softness than muscle. The woman was wearing a charcoal skirt with a silk maroon blouse, torn in a couple of places, and three-inch heels, which weren't exactly helping her as she tussled back and forth with the big guy.

The man didn't exactly seem attired for this sort of activity either. He was dressed more for a fancy restaurant, wearing a dark navy suit, with his jacket on, and even from several feet away I could make out the fancy cuff links on his French-cuff sleeves.

There was also a bright red palm print on the lady's left cheek. Other than that and the dishevelment of her clothing, she didn't seem too badly hurt yet. I sensed his patience was running out. Neither of them had noticed me, as far as I could tell.

At the moment I crossed the threshold, the guy reared back his arm, his hand deliberately cocked into a fist. He was red in the face, and if he connected with that punch it would be lights out, or maybe worse, for the Roberts woman.

I moved quicker than I have since retiring from the ring and had to dodge an overturned oak bar stool, probably what had made the crashing sound. The guy looked my way, his eyes popping in surprise. He had already committed to the punch, and it was whistling down towards the lady's face.

I reared my right arm up, blocking his forearm with my own, then powered on through and, arm to arm, wrestled him back onto the polished wood floor. It was hard enough that his eyes glazed over, then rolled up into his head.

With the big man out of the action for a while, I turned to Karyn Roberts. She was doing her best to rearrange her blouse and cover as much of her upper torso as possible. She blew her bangs out of her eyes and let the blouse fall to her waist.

The two of us stood there for a moment, she staring my way. I kept one eye on her and one on sleeping boy.

"You're welcome," I said.

"Yeah, thanks." She took a couple of more deep breaths. "Sorry if I seem ungrateful, but he just came at me out of the blue. I guess I'm kind of in shock."

I looked her over but couldn't see any of the signs of an impending meltdown. If the lady was about to lose it, she managed to keep it hidden well enough. I had all sorts of questions running through my head, such as who the guy was, what she was doing here and whose house we were in.

At the moment, though, I didn't want to push her.

"Well," I said, "guess it's time to call the cops."

"I'm not sure you want to do that," the lady said.

"Really?" I arched my eyebrows. "I know you've been out of the crime biz for a while, Miss Roberts. But this sure looks like assault and battery to me, maybe even attempted murder or kidnapping."

She shook her head, and her expression made her look like a teacher talking to the dumbest kid in class.

"Believe me, Mr. Quinton, I'm well aware of what he tried to do. And all things being equal, I'd have been on the phone a second after he hit the floor."

"Yeah?" I asked, my nerves starting to tingle.

"But that's Carson Jackson lying there."

Even if the first name in and of itself didn't mean anything, the last name sure did. And judging by the man's age, I could hazard a guess as to his identity.

"Great," I said.

"Yep."

Terrific.

I'd just body slammed the son of a Superior Court Judge.

CHAPTER TWENTY-ONE

"**T**HIS YOUR HOUSE OR HIS?" I asked the lady, pointing at the -unconscious man on the floor.

"His."

"What about the car?"

"Belongs to a friend of mine. She's letting me use it while I'm in town."

"She have more than one car?"

"A couple. But it doesn't matter because she's spending a few days in Italy."

"Nice friend," I said. "You can't afford your own vehicle?"

She made a face at me. "Of course, I can. But I was planning on doing a bit of snooping around while I was in town. I didn't want some smart guy tracking down my ID by my license plate."

"Sure," I said. "Public relations executives always show up out of the blue and insert themselves into murder cases. Happens all the time."

Karyn frowned but didn't say anything. I had more questions now than when I'd entered the house and no time at the moment to shake them out of her.

"Which reminds me," I said. "Why were you tailing me tonight?"

Carson Jackson, if the lady was playing it straight with me and not working some kind of con, groaned and turned over on his left side. While his eyes remained closed, his breathing had sped up a bit, and he was only a few minutes away from waking up.

"Shouldn't we be getting out of here while we can?" the lady asked.

"Depends," I said, working to show more nonchalance than I felt. Assaulting a judge's family in their home wasn't exactly conducive to continued good standing for my license.

"On what?"

"On which of you is the good guy and which is the bad guy."

Karyn frowned at that and glanced down at the still-unconscious Mr. Jackson.

"Actually, I'm not sure which side he's on, but I can guarantee I'm one of the good guys."

"Any way of proving that?" I asked.

She frowned again, harder this time. I thought about smiling at her to loosen her up, but didn't want to find myself facing a harassment suit.

Jackson groaned and rolled back to his other side. His eyelids fluttered for a moment before closing again.

"Okay," I said, "why don't you and I get out of here. Big Ugly there's about to wake up."

She nodded in agreement, I took her hand and we skedaddled out the front door. I put her into the Corvette, gave her the address of my gym, told her I'd see here there in fifteen minutes.

"What about you?" she asked.

"Need to stick around and have a man to man with the judge's son."

The lady shook her head. "You don't want to go back in there. You could get in trouble."

"I'll be okay." I gave her one of my patented Blond Bomber grins. "I'm a tough guy. Tough guys don't get hurt."

She shook her head and gave me a look that said she wondered if she was conversing with an idiot.

"You're taking a lot on faith, aren't you? What's to stop me from just driving away and leaving you behind?"

"My winning smile? My awesome personality?"

She shook her head again.

"How about the fact that I know where you work and can track you down that way?" I asked.

"Okay, you've got me there. How about a compromise?" She glanced down at her torn clothing. "How about I swing by my hotel first and get into something a little more presentable, then head out to your place?"

"Deal," I said as I stepped back from her car. "I'll be there before too long."

She started up the engine and pulled away.

I stood there and watched as the 'Vette whipped down the street, around the corner and out of the cul-de-sac, then turned and went back inside the house.

I had some business to conduct with Jackson and wanted to do it quick before he woke up.

CHAPTER TWENTY-TWO

IT TOOK ABOUT TEN MORE MINUTES for Carson Jackson to wake up entirely. When he did so, he spent a couple of seconds looking around to get himself oriented. What he saw was the kitchen where he'd been getting rough with Karyn Roberts before I broke the little party up.

Then he looked closer and saw that he was wedged into a corner of the kitchen, opposite the stove. I sat on a small wooden chair across from him, about eight feet away, my gun hanging loosely in my lap.

Jackson blinked a couple of times before trusting himself to speak.

"Where's the reporter babe?" he asked.

What a sweet talker.

"The former reporter babe's gone," I said. "Flew the coop. It's just you and me for now."

He peered closer, shook his head, then grimaced at the thunderbolt that must have rocketed through his cranium. While I'd pulled the momentum of my move at the last minute, not wanting to actually hurt the guy, falling flat back on a solid floor is no fun.

Especially if you're not trained in taking falls.

I was trained, had spent a good chunk of my adult life taking falls on a surface not too much softer than that kitchen floor. I wouldn't have wanted to do it if I could avoid it.

Not that it was an age thing, as such. I'm forty-six after all, which at least isn't fifty; however, even in my prime taking bumps, as it's called, was never anything I did for fun.

Jackson looked down now and showed a little surprise.

"You didn't tie me up," he said.

"Nope."

His face scrunched some more. "Why not?"

I dawdled my gun a bit, keeping it pointed away from him. "Tying you up would have constituted forcible restraint, which a good prosecutor, and I'm guessing your mom knows one or two, could easily turn into a kidnapping charge. And I've got no desire to spend time in a federal pen."

He nodded, as if that made sense. "You're not holding me against my will?"

"Not at all," I said, at the same time swinging the gun's barrel a trifle more in his direction.

"But you've got me at gunpoint," he pointed out fairly reasonably.

"No, I don't. I'm just sitting here looking at the wall. The gun's not even pointed in your direction. How can I be holding you here?"

"Meaning I can leave whenever I want?"

"Of course." I swung the gun a bit closer his way.

He placed his palms on the floor and started to level himself up, then changed his mind and relaxed again.

"I get it. I'm not restrained and you're not holding a weapon on me, just happen to have it in the room, so there's no way you can be charged with anything."

Not for nothing was he a judge's son.

Actually, while he'd followed the line of reasoning I'd laid out for him, I wasn't all that sure how well it would stand up in terms of a legal argument. I wasn't thinking long term here. I only wanted to get through the next few minutes.

"How about answering some questions," I said, "and I'll get out of here."

Jackson glanced down at the gun again before looking back up at me.

"Do I have a choice?"

I nodded in as legally ambiguous a manner as I could.

"Go ahead then," he said.

I sat up a little straighter and angled my weapon farther away from him. "This your house?"

"More or less. I'm renting it from a buddy who was transferred overseas. He bought it a few years back as a long-term investment and didn't want to sell it."

A simple yes or no would have worked fine for me, but I let it go. "How exactly did you get Karyn Roberts here tonight?"

The puzzled expression came back to his eyes. "She didn't tell you?"

"We didn't have a lot of time to talk as I was hustling her out of here."

"Huh?"

I sighed and moved the weapon a degree back towards him. "Didn't want her around in case you woke up and decided to go for round two."

"Oh no, hey, no guy." Jackson actually scrunched even further back into the corner, something I hadn't thought possible. "You've got the wrong idea."

"Oh? Why don't you correct me then? What was I supposed to think when I saw you getting ready to punch her?"

Jackson's face reddened, and he stared down at the floor. "Okay," he said. "So I got a little out of hand. But I don't go around beating up women."

"Then why . . ."

"'Cause I thought she could tell me stuff. I wanted her to fess up."

"Seriously, Carson. Who the hell says 'fess up' anymore? And about what?"

He looked up at me and peered closer. It was actually about the first time he'd directly faced me since our little talk had begun. A light gleamed in his eyes.

"I'll be damned. You were in court this morning. The Hampton lady's hearing."

Now it was my turn to look confused. "Yeah? What were you doing there?"

"Wanting to find stuff out."

"Okay," I said, "this is starting to get a little too Abbot and Costello." His dubious look told me he didn't understand the reference. Kids these days. "Would you just tell me straight out what kind of 'stuff' you're trying to find out?"

He nodded and sat up a little straighter. Probably figured if I was going to shoot him I would have done it by now.

"It's about my mom."

"The judge," I said.

"Yeah. I think she's in some kind of trouble."

My breath caught for a second, and I had to force myself to calm down.

"Trouble?"

"Yeah. And it has something to do with the Hampton trial. You know, the first one. Way back when."

CHAPTER TWENTY-THREE

A S IT WAS BEGINNING TO LOOK LIKE A REAL MESS, I figured that three heads were better than one, even if one of them was Carson Jackson's. I hustled the younger man into my Cherokee, even though he didn't seem very keen on the idea, and headed back to The Blaster, where I hoped I'd find Karyn Roberts waiting for me.

Whether she'd followed through was a whole other matter.

Of course, I could have just called, but I wanted a little more time first to talk to Jackson before all three of us sat down.

Turns out he was the one who started up the conversation without any prompting from me.

"I didn't recognize you just from court," he said as we pulled out of the cul-de-sac and headed back toward the main stretch of Providence.

"Oh yeah?'

"Yeah," he replied. "I've seen you perform plenty of times. When I was a kid, I was huge into wrestling. My mom took me to St. Louis and KC for the shows every chance she got. Which wasn't much with her work schedule. I saw you wrestle in St. Louis a dozen times or so."

If the guy's intent was to make me feel all buddy-buddy toward him, it came up short. If he intended to make me feel even older than I already did, he succeeded. I wasn't sure which it was and figured time would give me an answer.

"When I was a kid," he continued, "I never would have dreamed I'd someday meet The Blond Bomber."

I've been retired from the ring a long time, and only a few people call me the Blond Bomber anymore. Either close friends I allow to, or those who could outrun me, tend to call me Blondie. Most days, I prefer just good old Sam.

"The Bomber's a long ways in the past," I said.

"Oh sure, Quinton, I know that. It's just that . . ." and he shrugged and let it drop.

I took a corner, which now had us on Broadway, heading straight toward downtown Providence.

Which either is or isn't saying much, depending on your point of view. Although one of the larger Missouri towns, Providence doesn't even come close in size to Kansas City or St. Louis. It's in the top five, though, for whatever that's worth.

Our annual, live-in population is a little over a hundred thousand as of the last census. Every year, right around the end of August, our population swells by some thirty to forty thousand when all the college kids show up.

One of the town's main industries, if not the main one, is education, and with the state's largest public university set smack dab in the middle of our downtown area, for three fourths of the year we have this huge influx of young people.

Not that we mind, most of the time. After all, it's all those young people who pump fresh economic blood into our system nearly year-round. Us locals tend to grumble quite a bit about certain aspects of student life. The most recent one is those damned e-scooters that keep popping up all over the place, littering our landscape like a horde of oversized locusts with handlebars.

Driving down Broadway, not even into the downtown area yet, I passed four or five clusters of young people, all guys except for one girl wobbling to keep her balance in four-inch heels, zipping every which way on e-scooters. They're supposed to stay off the streets and sidewalks, which naturally leads to the unanswered question of where the hell people are supposed to ride them.

All I know for sure is that since their arrival a year ago, driving through Providence has taken on the dimensions of a contact sport.

We made it to The Blaster in under twenty minutes, and as soon as I parked the Cherokee in my preferred spot, Carson Jackson and I hopped out and headed inside.

By this time of night, things at the gym were beginning to wind down. Our busiest times, as with most workout places, are early morning, late afternoon and early evening. Graveyard shifters getting off work, those with regular hours winding up their day, and younger clients taking a break from work or schoolwork. We usually also have a surge round about eleven to midnight before we close up at one.

Right now figured to be into that dead spot between early evening and late night, and entering through the front doors I saw only a handful of souls. All seemingly working out alone, mainly positioned around our section of cardio equipment.

Were I less confident of a guy, as Jackson and I crossed the main floor I'd have considered holding my breath. When I'd asked Karyn to come here and wait for me, I doubted she'd imagined that I'd be bringing her recent attacker with me. I didn't even know for sure if she'd followed my request, or merely taken off for who knew where as soon as she was out of sight.

Turns out I needn't have worried because as soon as I stepped in the place, Lisa Nolan, my manager, waved me over.

As I walked over to where Lisa, wearing dark purple gym pants with a light pink tank top, was spotting a fortyish man doing bench presses, Jackson followed me like a whipped dog.

"What's up?" I asked.

Lisa answered me without taking her eyes off the barbell she was spotting. "Woman came in to see you. Said you told her to come here? She's in your office."

I looked to Jackson and jerked my head in the direction of my office. He continued following me.

When I opened the office door and the two of us stepped inside, Karyn Roberts was far from silent. As soon as she saw

Jackson she leaped up from behind my old desk, where she'd been sitting and screeched.

"Karyn, calm down," I said.

She backed up against the wall, right under the display that held my old championship belt from my days with the Midwest Wrestling League and pointed a shaky finger at Jackson.

"What the hell's he doing here? Why isn't he arrested?"

"Because I didn't call the cops. Would you please sit down?'

I motioned Jackson to one of my client chairs and took the other one myself, not wanting to further escalate things by trying to evict Karyn from behind my desk.

She stared at the two of us for a minute longer, then sat down against the wall, keeping my desk between us.

She had indeed gone to her hotel, or some place, and changed her outfit. She now wore faded Levi's, a turquoise knit top and Adidas tennis shoes.

"I thought you were on my side," she said.

"If I'm on anybody's side it's Sheila Hampton's," I replied. "And I'm starting to think she needs as many people on her side as she can get. Why don't each of you tell me your story so I can figure out where everyone fits into the puzzle. Not to mention why ole Carson here was getting ready to whack you when I showed up."

Jackson looked a little pale at my choice of words, but I didn't know a better way to say it. "You first, Karyn. What's your interest in all this?"

"In front of him?"

"Why not? You have something to hide?"

She frowned, then leaned forward, placing her elbows on the desk and tenting her chin with her palms.

"Okay. I was on staff at the *Providence Star* when Sheila came up for trial back when."

"Right," I said. "And I'm guessing it was early in your career. You were learning the ropes?"

"Learning?" She chuckled at that. "If by learning you mean green as a cucumber, damned straight. I'd barely gotten off the obituary desk, which is where everyone started in those days, and next thing I know I'm ushered into the editor's office and he's assigning me to the Derek Hampton murder."

"Waitaminit," I said, something clicking in my head. "The murder? Not the trial?"

Karyn nodded her head for emphasis. "Right, this was only the morning after Derek's body had been found. I mean, they'd already taken Sheila in for questioning, and everyone expected her to be charged real quick, but it was long before they ever went to trial."

"Why?" I asked, noticing how quiet Jackson was being in the chair next to me.

"Why what?"

"Why did you get assigned to it? *The Star* isn't exactly *The New York Times* or anything."

"Of course not," Karyn said. "These days it's practically on life support."

"It wasn't back then. And even with a staff that fit a paper of its size, there had to be more experienced crime people. Why do you think they assigned you the gig?"

Karyn leaned back in my chair and relaxed a bit. "I'm glad you're wondering that, too. Back then I never even gave it a second thought. I was just excited at what I saw as my big break. But I've thought about it a lot since then, especially once I left the news business, and I don't actually have a good answer."

"Did anyone at the time make a stink about it? Any of the paper's veterans?"

She nodded emphatically. "You'd better believe it. A couple of the old-timers in particular had more than one knock-down-drag-out in Richard's office. Again, in retrospect, he could have easily justified assigning a couple of people to the story. Absolutely no way. He shut those old timers out."

"Richard?" I asked.

"Haskins. The city editor back then."

I thought all that through for a minute, while Jackson fidgeted even more beside me.

"What'd you think at the time? About those veterans and their complaints?"

A faint blush came to Karyn's face, and she partially turned away for a moment before turning back to me. "To be honest, at the time I thought they were a lot of embittered old farts who wanted to hold a woman down. Now, I realize how naïve I was."

"Naïve how?" I asked.

She took a deep breath and placed her hands flat on my desk. For a moment, she stared off into the distance, at some point far away from my office. Then she shook herself and turned back to me.

"It's pretty simple actually," she said. "I think I was somehow part of the frame."

"Frame?"

"To put Sheila Hampton away. To nail her for her husband's murder."

At my side, Carson Jackson finally stirred himself.

"You weren't the only one," he said.

CHAPTER TWENTY-FOUR

"**O**KAY," I SAID, "TELL US YOUR SIDE."
Jackson fidgeted a bit, twisting and twining his fingers back and forth in his lap. Despite his size and age, he looked more like a little kid than anything else. I waited, giving him an impassive stare while Karyn gave him a look that could have cut through metal.

"I wasn't trying to attack you," he said, without looking up at Karyn. "I just needed information, and I guess I got carried away."

Carried away didn't even begin to cover it, though for the moment I let it go. "How'd you two end up together?"

"She called me." Jackson looked up now in Karyn's direction. "Said she wanted to talk to me about the trial way back when. I said sure, come on over."

"Just like that?" I asked. "You get his number out of nowhere and give him a buzz?"

"I used to be a reporter, you know. And even though I left the business long before the digital age caught on, I've kept up. It's not that hard to track someone down, as you should know."

I let the dig at my profession slide as well, seeing as I was more interested in the larger story unfolding in front of me.

"Why?" I asked.

"Huh?"

"Why were you wanting to talk to Carson here? What exactly are you doing in town?"

She looked away, and her fingers started scratching at the desk-top. I waited for an answer.

When it came, it wasn't from her.

"She wants to see my mother," Jackson said.

I glanced his way. "Come again?"

"She wants to see my mother, talk to her about the trial."

I looked to Karyn for either confirmation or denial.

She gave me a blank face in return.

"That true?"

She nodded.

"Thought you were out of the reporting biz?"

"I was. I am," she said. "But I'm classifying this as unfinished business."

Something more there that I didn't have time to go into it just then. "She may have wanted an in with your mom," I said to Jackson, "but why'd you agree to meet? What did you want from her?"

"Some answers," he said, his voice lowering about half an octave.

Both Karyn and I looked confused at that.

"Answers to what?"

He paused, as if wanting to pick the exact words to use, then spread his hands in a "to-hell-with-it" gesture.

"I want to know what happened back then."

I felt like I was wrestling in the ring with the greenest rookie, someone who had to be taught, retaught, then retaught again the simplest moves. A large part of me wanted to reach out and slap Jackson up the side of the head.

"What's it matter to you?" I asked. "Did you know Sheila or something?"

Shaking his head, he stared down at the floor, as if seeking the answers down there.

"Then what?" Karyn Roberts, obviously not as accustomed as me to dealing with green rookies, almost shrieked.

He looked up then, some sort of strength growing behind his eyes.

"My mom's scared someone's coming for her," he said.

"Coming for her?"

"Coming to kill her," he said.

CHAPTER TWENTY-FIVE

I DIDN'T KNOW WHAT THE HELL I had hold of. The first thing I thought was to pass that nugget of information on to Bernie. If another participant in the original trial felt under the gun, so to speak, then Bernie had a right to know. It could be either a good or bad thing for Sheila's defense, depending on how it was spun and who did the spinning.

A glance at the clock showed that it was relatively early, just around eleven or so. Not too late for me to give Bernie a quick call, but I hesitated.

"How long's your mother been worried?" I asked.

"A while," Jackson said. "I live down in Springfield. We only see each other a few times a month. The last few weeks, whenever we talked on the phone she sounded kind of agitated."

A few weeks, I thought. In other words, just about when Sheila Hampton's conviction began to fall apart.

Jackson continued, "I just came out and asked her what was bugging her. She didn't want to get into it, only said enough for me to catch on that she was terrified about something. I told her I was taking a few days off and coming out here."

"You usually borrow your friend's house when you visit?"

He shook his head. "Naw, I usually stay in a hotel or at mom's. Wanted to stay there this time. I mean, if she's in some sort of trouble I wanted to be as close as possible."

"Why didn't you?"

Jackson shook his head, some sort of pain flickering in his eyes. "She said she didn't want me around. That there was nothing going on and I shouldn't bother coming. Then I heard about that lawyer getting killed last night, the one who prosecuted Mrs. Hampton. I figured that could have something to do with this problem of my mom's. So I drove out here without telling her."

Karyn wore a pretty dubious expression.

I personally wanted a couple of hours to go somewhere, lie down, and sort all this out but didn't figure I had any spare time. If Jackson was on the level, and if his assumptions were right, then Sheila Hampton, and by extension Bernie, were in something way over their heads.

"Your mom lives in town, right?" I asked.

"No, she moved down to Jeff City after dad died. She commutes in for work."

I glanced at the clock again. Jefferson City was only about twenty-five miles away from Providence, meaning it would be coming up on midnight by the time I could get out there. Not exactly the best of time to be calling on a stranger.

"I'm going to head out there tomorrow," I said. "I think talking to her as quickly as possible would be good. I need you to go along to smooth the way for me."

"Whatever, man," Jackson said. "As long as she doesn't get hurt."

I had a hunch that the judge was fairly safe for the moment, but didn't want to give the guy any false hope.

"Give her a call," I said, "and tell her we're coming out first thing in the morning."

"I'll get a taxi to take me back home," he said as he pulled out his phone.

I looked at Karyn. "Where are you staying?" I asked. "We need to get together tomorrow."

She gave me the name of her hotel. I asked her if she wanted us to drop her off. She said she'd settle for an Uber, then went off a ways to make her own call.

I stood there alone, in my darkened gym, and I wondered again if I should call Bernie and give him a heads up.

Mentally flipping a coin, I decided it could wait until the morning.

A decision, as it turned out, that I was going to regret.

CHAPTER TWENTY-SIX

MY SECOND DAY ON THE HAMPTON CASE began with a hitch. Rather than go home to my apartment then turn around and come back, I'd stayed the night at The Blaster, sacked out on the couch in my office. I'd woke up, showered, grabbed a couple of donuts and dressed. Considering that I was going to be calling on a judge, an esteemed one at that, I decided to up my wardrobe a bit. When Carson Jackson showed up shortly before six, I was wearing my usual Levis, a light green polo shirt and a light silk blazer.

Jackson didn't look happy at all.

"I tried calling my mom," he said right away. "Couldn't reach her."

I glanced at the clock on my desk. "What time does she get up?"

"Usually around seven or so. Court usually starts at nine, if she has a case that day. Whether she has a case or not, she usually tries to get in around eight thirty or so," he answered.

"Did you call her after we split up last night?"

The guy actually glanced down at the floor and mumbled.

"I didn't get ahold of her," he said.

I gave him a look.

"Why not?"

"Well," the guy was almost literally ringing his hands, "she's getting up there, you know. And by the time I got back to my place I figured she'd already be in bed. Figured it wouldn't hurt to wait till this morning."

"But now you can't get her," I said.

"Uh, yeah."

"Christ, dude. Does she have a landline?"

"Yeah."

"You try that?"

"Both that and her cell. Nothing. You think I should have called the cops?"

I didn't want to tell the guy what I really thought. That if he hadn't been able to reach his mom last night, calling the cops now wouldn't do a whole hell of a lot of good.

I could think of all sorts of reasons the judge may not have answered her phone the night before. She could simply be an insomniac and took something to help her sleep.

Simple, sure.

And harmless.

I could also imagine all sorts of not-so-harmless possibilities, and there was no reason to waste time before checking them out.

"Let's go," I told the judge's son. "We'll take my car."

Heading south out of Providence, there's two main ways to get down to the capitol. Most people take the main U.S. highway to the east of town, which gives a straight shot right into Jeff. In fact, I'd say it's safe to assume that the majority of Providence residents, especially shorter-term ones, think that's the only way to go.

But if one has the time, and is in the mood for a little sight-seeing, there's a much curvier, hillier road that runs along the west side of town, snaking its way through a handful of villages and lots of farming land before eventually terminating right at the northern edge of the capital. However, between the steep hills, and even steeper declines, and all the curves and twists, this other route takes a lot longer to get there than the straight shot of the major highway.

The scenery makes the extra time more than worth it. However, especially considering Jackson's lack of communication with his mom and the overall urgency of our mission, the straight-line highway was much more preferable.

At first, as Jackson and I climbed into the Cherokee I automatically planned to head down that way. When he gave me his mother's address, I reconsidered. From various cases I've had over the years, I'm almost as familiar with Jeff City as I am with my own town, and the address Jackson gave me was far to the west, almost out into the country.

Either direction would have been six of one/ half a dozen of the other. I mentally flipped a coin and came down in favor of the main highway. Pulling out of the parking lot of the strip mall which contains my gym, I glanced over at Jackson.

He was on his phone and frowning.

"Well?" I asked.

Shaking his head, he spoke without looking my way, still staring out the window. "No answer," he said.

I looked out the window. The sun was just beginning to pink-up the eastern sky, and my stomach tightened when I considered the situation.

"She have any reason for not spending the night at home?"

He turned to look at me, obviously not finding whatever he was looking for out on the road. "My dad died about five years ago. Liver cancer."

Under ordinary circumstances, I'd feel like an ass for asking the next question, but it had to be done.

"She have male friends?"

Jackson shook his.

"One or two. Nothing serious."

"That you know of."

He frowned again and peered at me in the gloom of the Cherokee's cab. "Meaning what?"

"You live a hundred miles away, see her a few times a month. It's not inconceivable she has a man in her life you don't know about," I said.

He flicked his head. "Okay, as far as I know there's no one."

"Where is she on an early weekday morning?" I asked.

Jackson's shoulders hunched up. "Should I call the cops and ask them to go check on her?"

By this time, we'd gotten to the highway and had at least forty-five minutes to go until we could get out to the judge's place.

Sure, I thought, call the cops. And tell them what? That Jackson was worried about his mommy? That wouldn't go over very well at all. She was an active state judge, and it wasn't inconceivable that something had happened to her connected with her work.

Plus, there was the recent publicity around Sheila Hampton's conviction reversal and the subsequent murder of Robert Harris. If Jackson mentioned those names, it could get some sort of movement going on the cops' end.

Or maybe not. When it came down to it, we'd have nothing solid in the way of concerns. For all we knew, the judge had decided to take the day off work and sleep in.

In the end, though, better safe than sorry.

"Yeah," I said. "Call them, and let them know that we're on our way. Ask them to do a welfare check on her."

"Will they do it after only a few hours?"

"Probably not, but nothing says we can't give it a shot. Besides, she's not exactly an ordinary citizen."

Odds were that the local cops would get there a lot quicker than I would. My gut felt tight as I pressed down on the accelerator.

CHAPTER TWENTY-SEVEN

IT WAS A NICE HOUSE, though not what you'd call lavish. Even in the early morning dark, as I swept the Cherokee into the driveway, negotiating my way around a Jeff City patrol car with red and blue strobes flashing, I could tell a lot about the place.

Two stories, with an attached garage that looked large enough to hold three vehicles. A flagstoned walk led a couple of different directions, from the driveway up to the house and from the house to the garage door. The house itself was a pale blue with dark gray trim and balconies for two of the upstairs rooms. Even had a small version of a widow's walk off to one side of the roof, which had to be purely for effect, as the closest oceans were around eight hundred miles due south.

More than anything, the home whispered of ambivalence. It could have been owned by a family who'd started out poor and through hard work and tenacity managed to climb into the upper middle class, or it could just as easily have been the residence of someone definitely on the wealthy side who wanted to downplay their success.

Before I turned off the Cherokee, I could see in my headlights a slender, middle-aged woman wearing a pink robe talking with two uniformed cops. She stood about five feet even and had a nice mix of salt and pepper hair.

One of the cops, a young black woman, looked our way as Jackson and I exited the Cherokee.

"You fellows need something?" she asked. Before we could answer, Lois Jackson, who I recognized from occasional news stories here and there, glanced over at us.

"Carson? Do you have something to do with this?"

"Mom, I just wanted . . ."

As the two of them began talking to each other, I turned to the young cop and showed her my license. She peered at it for a second before handing it back.

"What's going on here, Mr. Quinton?" she asked.

So far her partner, a red-headed guy who looked to be about thirty, hadn't said anything.

"We were concerned for Judge Jackson's safety. Is everything okay?"

"Everything except for the fact that the judge there is royally pissed at the two of us. But wouldn't you be if you were yanked out of bed at the crack of dawn for no good reason?"

"She wasn't answering her phones," I said.

"She's a sound sleeper. Said she had the day off and wanted to sleep in. You want to make a federal case out of that?"

"Then there's no sign of any disturbance? Anyone trying to get in? Anything like that?"

The young cop peered closer at me, and I could almost see the cogs turning in her head. She kept her face expressionless though.

"We haven't had a chance to look real good, but everything seems on the okay." Her eyes narrowed. "You haven't answered my question, sir. What exactly is the problem here?"

I glanced over and saw the two Jackson's going at it. The judge, who had her hands on her hips and was glaring up as her son tried to explain.

I decided a little white lie wouldn't hurt all that much.

"The guy's been concerned about his mom's safety lately. Since his dad died, he worries about her."

"And he had you check her out?" Her face looked almost as skeptical as mine would have were our situations switched.

I shrugged. "He overreacted. We're poker buddies now and then and he called me up for help."

"Damned nice thing to do for a poker buddy." She didn't even try to hide the skepticism from her tone.

"Well, he did offer to throw a Franklin my way if I came with him."

"Uh huh." The cop, done with me, turned and began whispering with her partner. A minute later, she turned back to me.

"You wouldn't happen to know a Lieutenant Santiago up in Providence, would you?"

I plastered a smile on my face, one I didn't actually feel at the moment.

"Who, Bill? Sure do."

"Funny thing," the lady cop said. "He called us just a minute or two before the two of you showed up. Wanted to know if everything was okay out here."

"Bill's a good man."

"Sounds like. What I don't get is why a Providence cop is interested in a little domestic call down here, or how he knew about it."

I was kind of wondering the same thing myself. I was saved from trying to come up with a quick one when the judge and her son broke apart and came over our way.

It took another few minutes for things to get untangled. Once Judge Jackson assured the uniforms she was fine, and that yes, this was her son standing next to her, though she had no clue yet who I was, they took off.

Looking faintly disgruntled at having their time wasted, but not wanting to mouth off in front of a judge.

As they drove away, the judge herself turned to both me and Carson, her mouth pursed in the hardest frown I'd seen in years.

"Inside," she said, "and you two had better be ready to tell me what this is all about."

CHAPTER TWENTY-EIGHT

"**O**KAY, TALK," JUDGE LOIS JACKSON SAID as soon as we stepped into the house. She stopped barely six feet into the living room and turned our way, hands on her hips.

The living room itself pretty much matched the house's exterior. About thirty by forty feet, with an open doorway on the opposite end that looked like it led into the kitchen. The furniture was all broken-in brown leather and dark oak. An ornate fireplace, all old-looking brick and brass accessories, occupied the center of one wall.

The wall opposite the fireplace held several family photos, some of them showing the judge, a man I assumed to be her late husband, and Carson at varying stages of their lives. As the three of us stood there, a dark brown Welsh Corgi scampered into the room, took one look at me, and scampered right back out.

"Well," her son began, but she cut him off at the knees.

"Not you," she snapped, twisting a couple of inches my way, "him."

I'd been in the lady's presence all of five minutes, and I already knew one thing for sure. No way in hell would I want to mess up in her courtroom.

"Where you want me to start?" I asked.

"How about your name? And what you're doing with my son bothering me first thing in the morning?"

"My name's Sam Quinton and I'm . . ." A slight gasp and a frown from the woman cut me off.

"I've heard of you," she said, her brows slightly furrowed. "A detective, right?"

"Yes, ma'am." My mind zipped into overdrive. I'd been an investigator in Providence for going on five years now, long enough to have crossed paths with the good judge, but it never had quite happened. Even though she was still presiding in Carson County, my work hardly ever took me inside the courts building, and I'd never had cause to enter her room.

Hell, I knew more lawyers and clerical folks from them working out at The Blaster than I did from my other work.

The judge was giving me an ever-closer once over.

"You don't look like most private detectives I've met."

"Oh no?"

"No. Most of them are balding ex-cops with beer bellies hanging over their belts. You look more like a motorcycle thug."

The lady was looking for a fight, but I was there for information. I gave her my "aw shucks" grin, a look I'd perfected back in my ring days. I'd use the "aw shucks" to let an opponent know I really thought he was a great guy and put him at ease right before I smashed him over the head with a steel chair.

The "aw shucks" also worked quite well in the months after my divorce when I wanted to get in good with some cute young thing sitting across from me in a bar or club.

However, even confronted with the "aw shucks" the judge continued glaring.

Maybe the "aw shucks" grin had an age limit for effectiveness.

"I'm starting to thin out a bit on top," I said. "If that helps."

"I'm not in the mood for humor, young man. What's this big emergency that brings you and my son out here?"

Okay. The easy way wasn't going to work. Time to get hard.

"How do you know my name?" I asked, putting a bit of steel in my tone.

"Excuse me?"

"You know who I am and what I do. How's that? We've never met."

"I'm a judge. You don't think I'm familiar with . . ."

"Uh uh. I've never had cause to be in front of your bench."

"Well, then, I must have remembered your name from when you were in the news earlier in the year. During that whole organized crime mess back in the spring."

"Maybe," I said. "And that would kind of make sense. But I'm guessing that you've heard of me a lot more recently."

The judge tossed her head at that and, without even looking much at her son, walked over and sat down on the leather sofa.

"Regardless, what's this big problem you and Carson think I have?"

I ambled over myself and took a seat in one of the easy chairs that faced across from the couch. The judge frowned at that. Whether from the fact she hadn't offered me a seat or that she wasn't used to people in blue jeans and polo shirts lounging in her furniture, I wasn't sure.

"What are you afraid of, judge?" I asked.

She blanched, then recovered almost instantly. "I don't know what you mean, Mr. Quinton."

"Sure you do." I waved my hand to encompass her entire living room. "From where I'm sitting I can spot at least four concealed weapons, hidden away in various nooks and crannies." In my peripheral vision, I saw Carson looking confused. "I'm telling you, judge, if you have someone after you, you're going to have to do a lot better than .22's and .38's. I'm guessing you know how to shoot, right?"

Her demeanor had taken on an extra layer of frostiness, something I hadn't thought possible. "My home décor isn't any business of yours, young man. But for what it's worth, yes, when I was a prosecutor I took a shooting course at the police academy. I was dealing with some rather unsavory cases at the time."

I nodded as if that made perfect sense. "And I'm guessing that these days you don't have guns stashed all around the house on a regular basis."

The lady continued to look fiercely at me. Her son had become an afterthought to this entire conversation. "What's your point, Mr. Quinton? And make it quick, then get out of my house."

"It's just that I'm seeing a pattern here, judge. A quarter century ago, Sheila Hampton was sent to prison for life for murdering her husband. Then, just a week ago, she's released, her original conviction thrown out. I'm sure you heard about that?"

"I don't need the sarcasm, mister. You know damned good and well I was kept in the loop as all of that went down. But it's nothing to do with me."

I raised an eyebrow at that. I wouldn't have kept my skepticism off my face even if I could have. "Nothing to do with you, judge? Seems to me it has a whole lot to do with you. After all, if you ran such a lousy trial that . . ."

She jumped to her feet, her face taut and practically clenching her fists. Jackson, off to the side, shifted a bit.

I continued ignoring him.

"There was nothing wrong with that trial!" the judge snapped. "I ran it right down the line. If the appellate court saw anything wrong on my part they would have . . ."

"Then," I worked to keep my voice calm, though the lady was starting to worry me a bit, "just a few days after Sheila's release, Robert Harris gets knocked off, and the prevailing theory is that Sheila came looking for revenge after a wrongful conviction."

"Out of my house!" Lois Jackson's voice cracked on the last word. "Get out and don't you dare . . ."

"Which is what has me puzzled," I interrupted her, unruffled. "The cops picked up Sheila almost immediately, and she's been held in jail ever since, denied bail. What are you so afraid of?"

She stood in place, almost frozen, veins etched on her face. "I've heard enough of this. I want you gone, now."

Off to the side, her son's mouth opened and closed like a fish gasping in air. Hard to believe that just a few hours before he'd been such a tough guy slapping Karyn Roberts around. Figuring my point was made, I stood up.

"Harris was the prosecutor on the Hampton case, a star-making case if there ever was one, and he never moved much up the ladder. You were the judge on that case, and you also didn't do a whole lot better than you had before. All these years later, and you're stuck in state court. Howard Landon was the defense attorney, and he was pretty much a broken man afterwards. Tell me, judge, what went on in that trial that was so awful? Had to be something more than just an innocent woman being railroaded."

When I finished, silence filled the room. Judge Jackson's eyes were practically distended. I had a hunch that the emotion flooding her wasn't the surface anger she projected, but some sort of deep, lurking fear. It took several heartbeats before she got herself even partially under control.

Then, just as she began to breathe normally again, I turned things up another notch.

"Actually, the more I dig into all this I can kind of understand it. I'd guess that George and Mary Hampton were probably pretty pleased with how things turned out."

"I don't know what you—"

"Little brother dead, his widow sent up for life. They would have walked away with their company and, since Derek and Sheila didn't have any children, the bulk of Derek's personal fortune. Yep, I can see how they'd be willing to show their appreciation."

I was spitballing. Throwing things out there without any foundation and hoping something scored.

But I wasn't sure I'd succeeded. The lady turned an even deeper shade of red, which I wouldn't have thought possible.

"I'm not going to stand here and be slandered by some has-been jock. You have one more chance to get the hell out of my house before I call those cops back and have them haul you off. Understand?"

I glanced at her, if I'd been wearing a hat I would've tipped it, and started moving to the door.

"No problem, judge. I'm guessing Carson and you here have some talking to do. I'll just see myself out."

As I left the house, I knew that, despite seemingly a bust, I'd at least come away with one nugget of information. I couldn't disagree with the judge's assessment of me as a "has-been jock," but it was curious.

She must have known a lot more about my background than she'd originally let on.

It was definitely time for me to update Bernie Lyman.

CHAPTER TWENTY-NINE

Turned out my call to Bernie would have to wait a bit. I'd barely pulled my Cherokee out of the judge's driveway before a familiar-looking dark blue Lincoln pulled up alongside of me.

Glancing out the window, I saw Marcus, along with several other faces crowded into the back of the Lincoln, staring back at me.

I briefly contemplated making a run for it then decided against it. I was beginning to get tired of these people. Hard to believe that only the morning before Bernie had interrupted my squats to tell me the sad tale of Sheila Hampton. I didn't feel up to a running car chase through the streets of the state capitol, incurring who knew what sort of risk to innocent bystanders.

I also toyed with pulling out my phone and making a quick call to 911, before discarding that idea in the next instant. If Marcus and his entourage were planning on doing me grievous bodily harm, it would be over and done with before any cops managed to show up.

Besides, what would it do to my tough guy rep if I went running for help every time some bad guys looked sideways at me?

I didn't see any possible moves besides the obvious one. While Marcus and his boys hadn't exactly waved their roscoes out the windows like gangsters from a black and white movie, the implication was pretty clear.

Like an obedient little pup, I weaved a bit to the side and pulled over to the curb, rolling down my window as I did so. We were in a residential area, and I hoped if fireworks started some concerned citizens would at least call the cops.

Marcus and one other guy, a big beefy black man, stepped out of the Lincoln.

"Mr. Quinton," Marcus said, "would you get out of the car please?"

"Why?" I asked, staying firmly in my seat.

The guy looked blank for a moment. He exchanged glances with his cohort.

"Because I'm asking you to," he said after a moment.

"Why?" I repeated.

"Excuse me?"

"I'm driving down the street minding my own business. Sound familiar? And for the second time in two days you're ordering me around. Don't you think this is getting a little old?"

Marcus glanced again at the black man, then reached behind his back and pulled out a .45, though he kept it pointed toward the ground.

"Okay, old man, let's stop screwing around. Get out of the damned car."

The second guy hadn't moved. I wanted to crane my head around and try to get an accurate count of the other heads in the Lincoln, but now that Marcus had dropped all pretense I didn't dare take my eyes off him.

"You really need that for a has-been jock?" I asked.

"Huh?"

"That's how Judge Jackson referred to me, has-been jock. Since you and she are such good buddies, I figured you'd feel the same way."

"What the judge and I are is none of your concern, Quinton. It seems you didn't understand what my employers were telling you just yesterday. Now get out of the car."

He hadn't yet leveled the gun at me, and his compatriot was as motionless as a statue, looking neither bored, concerned nor excited, almost as if waiting for a stray breeze to come by and bring him to life.

"Won't the Hamptons mind if you start shooting up this quiet little street?" I asked. "Because otherwise, I'm not sure how you're going to get me to exit my vehicle."

Marcus smiled, shook his head, and took a step closer to my car. "You can't be this stupid, Quinton. Do you not realize who you're messing with?"

"Let's say I get all knock kneed and jittery and climb out of this car. What's going to happen?"

"Maybe I just want another shot at talking to you."

"Not the best choice of words," I said. "Besides, seems to me we're talking right now."

Marcus said. "Or maybe me and the boys are going to kneecap you, stomp you into the pavement and leave you bleeding out."

A pro wrestler is as much an actor as an athletic performer. There's a term used in the business, called "selling," which is when your opponent pulls some move or hold on you that's supposed to hurt like hell, even to the extent of actual injury, and you go with it. Grimacing, groaning, sometimes even screaming, to let the crowd know that you are, in fact, hurting worse than they can possibly imagine, when actually at the worst you're getting a good tickle.

But a good seller doesn't just work in the moment. Let's say your opponent has been working on your knee and performed a move that looks as if it would hobble an ordinary person. For the rest of the match, if not beyond, you have to continue to act as if that knee is about to give out on you. These days, while everyone in the audience *knows* that you're not actually hurt, you have to perform as if you are.

You have to sell it.

Right about now, I was selling like crazy. Mainly because, if my pal Marcus and his buddies wished it so, I was only a couple of minutes away from being maimed, if not killed outright.

I had to look as if I was the one holding all the cards, as if, no matter what, I was going to be walking away high and dry.

I just hoped my selling skills were up to the task.

"I don't think your heart's into going that route," I said to the Hamptons' errand boy.

"Don't push me, Quinton. You weren't that tough back in your prime, and you're facing real tough guys now."

"What's to stop me from just waving to you and driving away?

"What do you think?" he asked as he shifted his .45 just enough to line up with my front tire.

"I don't think your employers would like that," I said.

"What the fuck all do you know about them?"

"I know they like to keep things quiet. Whatever the hell's going on here, they've kept it shushed for over twenty years. And if Amendment V hadn't come along and gotten Sheila out of prison, it would still be quiet."

Marcus glared at me but didn't say anything, and I hoped I'd pegged the situation correctly.

"All of which makes me wonder what you're doing out here this morning," I continued. "Seems to me awfully coincidental. I visit Judge Jackson and you just happen to show up. What's it going to be, guys?"

I raised my right hand, which had been down in my lap, and rested my own weapon on the window frame. "We going to throw down or what?"

I have no way of knowing how long I would have been willing to keep the standoff going, but I kept my gun focused squarely on Marcus. It wouldn't prevent his men from saying the hell with it and unloading on me. I just hoped it would at least forestall things a bit.

A couple more heartbeats went past, and Marcus took a step backwards. The big black guy by his side, who hadn't yet said a word, mimicked his move.

"Don't get too cocky there, Quinton. You don't know the kind of people you're dealing with, but if you keep this up, you'll find out."

He and his buddies holstered their weapons, climbed back into the Lincoln and drove away.

I waited until they'd been out of sight for about three minutes before I began breathing easily again.

CHAPTER THIRTY

B Y THE TIME I RETURNED TO PROVIDENCE it was around eight. I considered calling Bernie and filling him in on what had gone down, but I hadn't slept all that well, or long, the night before, and the second confrontation with Marcus and his rat squad had shaken me up more than I wanted to admit.

I figured Bernie would be busy at the start of the day. A little more sleep felt like the thing to do, and by the time I hit Arena Avenue and took it towards Providence's downtown, I decided to head straight home.

I've got a nice apartment in a complex on the south side, and it took only a few minutes off the main highway to get there. I stopped to grab the mail from the day before, then made my way inside and collapsed on my couch, taking time only to strip my sport coat off.

I woke up a few hours later, stretched and had two quick cups of coffee, then showered, dressed and made my way to The Blaster. By this time, the gym had been open for a while, and as I walked in I saw several clients moving around the front part. I didn't know who was down to be in this morning, either Lisa or Keri Eckland. Either way, the place was in good hands.

My couple of hours of sleep hadn't done much to straighten things out in my head, and I felt a bit grumpy. I decided to do what a lot of guys do when they have a mental problem, indulge in a good workout. Bernie had interrupted me doing my squats the day before, and for various reasons I hadn't had a really good workout in a couple of days. And with Mike Palmer, Judge Jackson, Karyn Roberts and my recent encounter with the Hamptons, I had quite a bit to think about.

Turned out, though, that I wasn't going to get started on that workout for a while. I was only halfway across the front part of the gym, heading to my office to get into my gear, when Lisa, clear-eyed and wearing a sky-blue workout suit, came up to me.

"You're popular this week," she said.

I gave her a blank look.

"In your office," she continued. "I made sure everything was locked up before I let him in there."

"Let who in?"

"Said he was from the State Troopers," she said before grabbing a towel off a rack and heading over to help a fiftyish woman struggling with one of the treadmills. I walked back to my office.

I opened it right away, not bothering to knock or announce myself in any way. I saw a small, compactly-built man with thick red hair sitting in one of my client chairs, his right leg crossed over the left.

"Sam Quinton?" he queried as I walked in. I nodded, went to my small refrigerator and grabbed a small bottle of ginger ale.

I opened the refrigerator door to show him the limited selection I had and raised an eyebrow. The man shook his head. Closing the door, I sat down behind my desk and took a good look at him.

He was one of those guys whose age is hard to pin down. Although his face had lines, they were good lines, what my granny used to call character lines. He had most of his hair, with only a little of it gray. The guy could have been anywhere from thirty-five to fifty-five and I wouldn't have been surprised.

"How may I help you?" I asked.

He reached into his pocket and pulled out a small badge case. Flipping it open, I saw both a badge and an ID card for Sergeant Wilson Prescott of the Criminal Investigation Division of the state highway patrol.

"Darn," I said, "that almost looks like the real thing."

The man put his badge back in his pocket and sat back down.

"What makes you think it isn't?" he asked.

"For one, you don't look like a Wilson. And Prescott is a name that belongs to a Canadian Mounty, not a Missouri trooper."

My visitor sat composed, not even ruffled by my, admittedly lame, humor. "I hear you used to be some kind of showman, Quinton."

I smiled and pointed to the heavyweight belt hanging behind my desk. "Some kind of one."

"Obviously not very successful," he commented.

Ouch. The dude had comeback.

"And I assure you," he continued, "that my badge and ID is absolutely real. You don't believe so, keep screwing with me and you'll see just how real it is."

I placed my hands out, palms forward. "What can I do for you, sergeant?"

"Your name isn't exactly unknown to us," Prescott said, "mainly because of the Lipardo/ O'Brien thing a while back. You caught some attention with that one."

"That was mainly Josh Nichols at work."

Prescott shook his head. "Sgt. Nichols had his contribution, of course. But informal sources say it all would have gone to hell without you."

I put on my humblest grin, which caused zilch reaction with Prescott.

"And now," he said, if anything looking annoyed at my earlier attempt of a grin, "you're taking on George and Mary Hampton."

I had a hunch where this was going and sobered up my expression. "What the hell is this? Does everyone in this town have me wired?'

"More than you may think," Prescott said, "but no one else is my concern. What's your business with Judge Lois Jackson?"

"Who's asking?" I shot back.

"I already showed you my . . ."

"No," I said, interrupting him, "who's really asking? Our new lieutenant already gave me his two cents worth on this, and now you? You going to tell me that a sergeant came all the way here from the capital, or wherever you're located out of, to pry into my business?"

"All the way here is something like twenty miles," he pointed out, "as you know because you made the trip just this morning."

I took a deep breath, gauging how to respond. Among other things, I was conceivably only a few minutes away from losing my investigator's license.

I waved that away. "You know what I mean. You didn't decide this on your own. So who sent you?"

Prescott gave me a stare that no doubt worked fine on most regular cons. In fact, it worked pretty good on me, though I just barely managed not to show it.

I think.

It occurred to me that for the second time in less than twelve hours someone was trying to muscle me away from the judge.

"Let me put it this way, Mr. Quinton. A few hours ago, Judge Jackson called someone fairly high up in state government, who then called my lieutenant, who then called me. The judge says you threatened her in her home. Why not think of me as just the messenger. You are to steer clear of any and all activity that involves Judge Lois Jackson, or you'll have to find a new line of work. Is that clear?"

I thought it over a minute before answering. "No."

"Excuse me?" A slight shade of red had come over the sergeant's face.

"I said no, it's not clear at all. What exactly was I supposed to threaten the judge about? And did she mention that her son was with me at the time?"

"Okay, mister . . ."

"Far as that goes, did she file a formal complaint? Or is this just an informal how ya doin'?"

Prescott leaned forward in his chair. I had the impression that if we hadn't been sitting down with my desk between us, and I didn't have about five inches on him, he would have considered poking a finger in my chest.

"At the moment it's informal, mister. But if you want, this can get real official real quick. Down at headquarters, we kind of hold a dim view of people threatening state judges."

"Me too," I said.

"Huh?"

"I'd take a dim view of it, too. Which is why I didn't do any such thing. Seems to me the best thing to do here would be for the judge to go on the record, you guys file charges against me, and we let the lawyers sort it all out. I know my attorney wouldn't mind the extra work. How about it? Let's get the ball rolling."

Now the sergeant leaned back, slight confusion creasing his face. "I don't know quite what you're thinking, Quinton, but . . ."

"What I'm thinking is that there's an awful lot of people jumping on me in the last twenty-four hours since I went to work for Sheila Hampton. And I'm also starting to wonder just what it is that everyone wants to keep hidden. Why don't you go ahead and file a complaint, haul me off, lock me up, whatever it is you want, and then Bernard Lyman can start taking everyone to the cleaners."

Prescott stood up, his face more flushed than it had been a moment before.

"You don't know what you're asking for, bud. I may just be a sergeant, but there are some people who could have your license yanked in nothing flat."

"I've already gone a round with a lieutenant, and he wasn't any scarier than you are."

I stayed seated as the man turned and went to the door. As his hand grasped the knob, but before he opened the door, I spoke up.

"Sergeant." He glanced at me over his shoulder. "What'd Sheila Hampton ever do that has so many people against her?"

"From what I hear, she killed her husband."

"Appellate court says otherwise."

"No, Mr. Quinton. The appeals court says there wasn't enough for a conviction the first time around, not that she didn't do it."

He had me there.

"Well, have a nice day. And tell your bosses that Bernie Lyman and I said hey."

The trooper's face flushed even more as he slammed out of my office.

I didn't know much about his little visit, though there was one thing I felt pretty safe assuming.

No way had the guy been here on official business.

CHAPTER THIRTY-ONE

AFTER PRESCOTT HAD LEFT, I didn't feel much like working out. I called and left a message for Nichols, asking him to check on something for me. At the moment, I figured it as fifty/fifty as to whether he would, but didn't hurt to make the old try.

I sat at my desk for a while, shuffling papers mindlessly, then decided to head out to try to catch Bernie at his office. I called before leaving and talked to one of his associates, who told me that Mr. Lyman was in conference with a client and couldn't be disturbed.

That confused me for a minute. When had Sheila Hampton managed to get out of jail? Then I realized that, Sheila's notoriety notwithstanding, Bernie no doubt had other clients he was doing work for at the same time. Made me feel lucky in the fact that I handle, at most, one case at a time.

Then again, Bernie's tax forms are a hell of a lot more impressive than mine, and he only has one business compared to my two.

I stopped to let Lisa know I was going to be gone for a while and didn't know for sure when I'd be back. She nodded, without saying anything, and continued showing a gray-haired woman in her sixties how not to hurt herself while using an elliptical machine. As competent as Lisa was, and now that we'd hired Keri as an assistant, I could be gone for a year and no one would notice.

Stepping outside, I had a feeling that Indian summer had arrived. Barely nine o'clock, and the temp flashing on a bank marquee down the street said 82 degrees. I stepped off the sidewalk in the direction of my Cherokee, then paused.

I glanced around the parking lot, then up and down Arena Avenue. Everything looked normal and ordinary for a weekday morning. The strip mall's parking lot was about a quarter full, with most of the vehicles clustered close to the south end, where a donut shop and health food store abutted each other. The patch of lot outside of a local tax preparer's office was almost empty, no big surprise in early September, and the rest of the cars, SUV's and pickups were scattered around the rest of the area.

No dark blue Lincolns lurking around, which I took as a good sign.

On Arena, the early morning traffic sped by on its usual course. Between the four lanes and all the turn bays, bicycle lanes and side streets, nothing looked out of the ordinary.

No roving band of state troopers ready to pounce on me, haul me off in cuffs and strip me of my license.

Okay. I was being a little paranoid. Yesterday's events would do that to a guy, even one as tough and rugged as me.

Though tough and rugged doesn't get you far when the cops head your way with their tasers leveled.

Shaking my head at my own foolishness, I stepped off the sidewalk and headed to my car.

"I DON'T FUCKIN' BELIEVE IT."

"I hope you don't use that type of language in court," I said.

"Never mind what I say in court. Go over that last part again, will you?"

I repeated what I'd already told him a minute before about the visit from the trooper. Bernie quietly hummed and hawed while I did so, and when I finished he sat there staring off into space.

After a few minutes, I'd had enough. "Bern?"

He snapped his eyes back to me. "Sorry, Sam. Was working it through in my head. I'd say it's safe to say that something's up."

"I hate to insult your great legal mind, Bern, but I'd already come to that conclusion. But what could be this big? Let's say Sheila got a lousy trial back when. Let's even say there was some kind of shenanigans going on. Is that possible?"

"I'd say likely. I'd never seen Howard Landon as frustrated in court as he was during that week. It almost seemed a foregone conclusion that the judge had made up her mind already."

"That's my point. Let's say the judge did. Let's say, for whatever reason, that the Hamptons reached out to her and made her throw the trial the prosecution's way. Where's the quid pro quo?"

"What do you mean?"

I spread my hands out in front of me. "If she helped throw the trial to the prosecution, what'd she get out of it? She continued basically at the same position ever since. She kept living in the same place, at the same standard of living. Her house looks, both inside and outside, about what you'd expect from someone of her pay level."

"You're saying she got nothing out of it?" Bernie asked.

"Right."

"Maybe she just thought Sheila was guilty."

"Anything in her past record to show to show she'd be amenable to any kind of corruption?"

Bernie considered that for a second, his brows furrowed.

"Not really," he eventually said. "She's always been known as an old-fashioned 'hang-em' type of jurist, though not so much that she ignores basic fairness."

"And yet, according to you, she was anything but fair during Sheila's trial."

"True, although not enough that she was obviously biased."

"What about Harris?" I asked.

"Harris? Blondie, you're getting confused. He's the victim, remember? The dead guy."

"I know that Bern. What I'm asking is, back during his time as a prosecutor, was he known for cutting corners? Any shady practices in court? Could he have known Sheila was innocent but moved full steam ahead anyway?"

Bernie took even longer to think that one over, his hand caressing his chin. "Again, not anything you'd call shady. He was tough to go up against. Most defense attorneys preferred to steer clear of him. But never anything really crooked."

"Until we get to the Hampton case."

Bernie shook his head. "I'm going to throw your own logic back at you, Sam. Say for a minute he knew Sheila was innocent and was working for someone to put her away. Why? What's the motive?"

"I'd say the Hampton fortune is a pretty strong motive. Plus, didn't you say something about Derek was the one actually running the business? Probably shouldn't discount good old sibling rivalry. And I'm guessing Sheila was the main heir, and since she couldn't profit from her crime, Derek's fortune went right to . . ."

"George and Mary naturally. Along with control of the companies. So what? It's not like they were destitute living on their shares. And again, after the trial was over Harris stayed right where he was. He even considered running for D.A. a couple of times but was talked out of it."

I mulled that one over for a minute. "Was he talked out of it" I asked, "or ordered to back off?"

Bernie gave me a look like someone had dropped me on my head.

"I don't quite get what you mean. As far as I know both, times friends of his pointed out it wasn't quite his time."

"He did end up going into private practice," I pointed out.

"Only a few years ago," Bernie said. "After he'd already retired as a prosecutor. And he took mainly a figurehead job. Winton and Burroughs took him on as a partner to up their private image."

"Lucrative?"

"Depends on how much they pull in each year. They're a decent-sized firm, though they don't have either the size or prestige to make someone commit malpractice just to get on with them two decades down the line."

I slumped in my chair, my brain going numb. "The two people most in a position to influence the trial, and get Sheila convicted, also don't seem to have profited by it in any way."

"That's about the size of it. What next?"

"Where do things stand legally?"

He plucked back the cuff of his sleeve to check the time, even though he had a clock sitting right on his desk. Probably wanted me to notice his Omega.

I think I've mentioned that Bernie saunters.

"I have an in-camera meeting in half an hour. Something about a new witness the prosecution's uncovered. Where do you go from here?"

"I'm thinking Harris," I said. "If we assume Sheila's smart enough not to kill someone she'd obviously be suspected of, that leaves the question of who did kill him and why."

"Just be careful," Bernie said as I stood up, "that you don't run into your friends again."

I cocked an eyebrow at him. "You mean the thugs, Lieutenant Santiago, or my buddy the state cop?"

"Either," Bernie said, "I'm expecting you to be a client of mine for a lot of years to come."

I cocked my hand into a gun shape and squeezed the trigger at him, then walked out the door.

CHAPTER THIRTY-TWO

WHILE THE OBVIOUS NEXT STEP was to check out Harris's workplace and office, I discounted that almost immediately. Under ordinary circumstances, if there was anything to be found there, the cops would have had it by now. Though possibly not in this case because once they'd quickly latched onto Sheila they appeared to have stopped looking entirely.

Which shows that sometimes we don't learn from experience. Almost the exact same sequence of events had happened two decades prior, and look how that turned out. Therefore, there was a good chance that Harris's office hadn't been searched. However, I seriously doubted if the partners in his firm were going to let me waltz in there and take whatever I wanted.

Besides which, if the man had anything in any way incriminating in his possession, he'd have been a total fool to keep it in his office.

A much more accessible avenue of information was the man's home although it stood to reason that this also had been, or was in the process of being, thoroughly examined by the cops. Whether they had or hadn't, as a private citizen I had absolutely no official call to invade the deceased man's privacy, even if it could potentially help Bernie's client.

Therefore, a shortcut was required.

Before pulling out of my parking spot, I pulled out my phone and placed a quick call to my shortcut.

After all we'd been through, no way my buddy would let me down.

"FORGET IT," JOSH NICHOLS SAID about two minutes later. "Absolutely no way."

"Come on, Josh. All I want . . ."

"All you want is for me to let you violate a private residence, and a crime scene at that, for no good reason. And this after your little stunt with the judge."

"What stunt?" I said because I couldn't think of a snappier comeback.

"Come on, Blondie. You don't think us dumb cops talk to each other? You were barely out of her driveway before the phone calls started in. Has anyone from the state guys visited you yet?"

"Maybe." I tried my best to put innocent disbelief in my voice.

"Uh huh," Nichols said, "which means yes. And you thought they weren't going to check you out with us? You want to hear a blow-by-blow description of the grief Santiago gave me a little while ago?"

"Not really. About Harris's home . . ."

"No."

"I have a good reason."

"Which is?"

"The man was murdered."

"Gee, thanks for the heads up."

"What I mean is . . ."

"What you mean is that you don't think we did a good enough job processing the scene. Right?"

"Depends."

A long moment of silence went by, and I could visualize Nichols counting to ten.

"On what?" he asked.

"On what you were looking for."

"Oh? Well please tell me, Blondie, what should we have been looking for?"

"Anything that would point to why he was killed."

"Gee, wish we'd thought of that."

"That ties into the Derek Hampton case," I added.

Now the silence stretched out even more.

"Sam . . ."

"I'm serious, man. Take off your cop hat for a minute and put on your private citizen hat. Doesn't this all seem just the least bit preposterous to you?"

"The Hampton thing was a quarter century ago."

"Or a few weeks back, depending on your point of view."

"You're implying that Harris's role in that was more than just that of a zealous prosecutor."

"No, I'm implying that this doesn't make a whole lot of sense. But let's run with that for a minute, okay? Let's say, just for the hell of it, that Sheila Hampton was framed and that, as the prosecutor, Harris had something to do with it."

"They found her with the body," Nichols pointed out.

"Run with me for just a second, guy. Let's say she was framed."

"Okay, I'll give you that. For a minute or two."

"Fair enough. Let's even go further and say that Harris was just a cog in a larger machine. If that's true, then Sheila getting released, even all this time later, could gum up the works."

"And the machine would start covering its tracks."

"Bingo. And everywhere I go I run into the Hamptons' bully boys."

"About that, the main dude's name is Marcus Leon."

"Leon? Seriously? Like in lion? That can't be a real name."

I could almost see Nichols shaking his head.

"Whether it is or isn't isn't really germane at this point."

"Germane?"

Nichols growled. "You want to hear this, or you want to keep nitpicking me about my grammar?"

"Sorry," I said in as subdued a tone as possible.

"As I was saying, Marcus Leon. Age, forty."

I grimaced, remembering how Marcus, who I'd guessed around thirty-five or so, had called me an old man. "He's a young-looking forty."

"I'll take your word for it. Record, in terms of incarceration absolutely clean. He did a stint in the military, even some time as a Ranger, before being cashiered out. Some sort of beef about requisitions at his base. The sheet doesn't go into any detail about exactly what he did."

"Which means it was something embarrassing to the brass above him."

"More than likely. Anyway, he cashiered out at twenty-five and put himself on the open market."

"Working for cartel or mob types?" I asked.

"Not so as you can tell. Mainly rich business people. Did bodyguard work, surveillance, whatever the job required that his skills fit."

"Any rough stuff?"

"Not in black and white," Nichols said. "But if you read between the lines, every now and then he may have gotten a little tougher than the law would allow."

I took a minute to think that through. In the background I could faintly hear shouted voices, heavy steps and the general hubbub I'd noticed on previous visits to the detective squad room.

I hadn't been up there in some time, and I guessed that Nichols still had his own desk. As a sergeant, his desk had been situated closest to the lieutenant's. Far as I knew, that's where he was located.

Thinking along that line reminded me of Santiago, and I felt kind of unsure about roping my buddy into helping me, less than a day after his new lieutenant had given me his version of the "be out of town by sundown" speech.

"Maybe that's a point," Nichols chimed in. "If this Leon character is working for the Hamptons, they may be dipping their toes over the line of legitimacy. I'll admit we weren't looking for that."

"Then let me. Give me some breathing room to go in and check Harris's place out. Is there a family at all around?"

"No family. He had a wife who passed away last year. No kids. And a sister who lives in St. Louis." He paused again, doing a lot of that this morning, before speaking back up. "No way, Sam. I'll send a few guys over to look through his things again, but no way I can sanction you."

"The new boss wouldn't approve?"

"Yeah, I heard you and the lieutenant went a round or two. He told me all about it this morning."

"Did he tell you I won him over with my charm and made him a fan?"

"No, he said you were a self-delusioned prick who didn't know when to leave well enough alone."

"He did? He was a lot nicer in person."

"I paraphrased."

"Josh," I said, lowering my voice a bit, "if Harris was corrupted in some way, who's to say you can trust whoever you send over." I thought of all the money, all the power at the disposal of the Hamptons. "Odds are the machine didn't just have the one cog."

He began breathing heavy, and for a moment I thought he was going to yell at me again. Then the exhalations died down, and when he spoke his voice was back to normal.

"Forget it, Blondie. I'm going to play a hunch and send a few guys over to go through his place again. They'll get there around five or so. Middle of the afternoon at the earliest. You stay the hell away. Understood?"

I smiled, even though he couldn't see me over the phone.

"Understood."

CHAPTER THIRTY-THREE

FOR THE LAST YEAR OF HIS LIFE, since the death of his wife, Robert Harris had lived in a condominium in a relatively new subdivision in the northwest area of Providence called Silver Estates. The name conjured up images of elderly people living in near-mansions. The truth was a bit off of that. As I pulled the Cherokee under an arched wooden structure that spelled out the development's name in six-inch high letters, I shook my head.

No doubt some senior citizens lived in the Estates; however, the sparsity of vehicles at the noon hour implied that the majority of residents were out working. Even the "estates" part was a bit of a stretch, as most of the structures within view took the form of mid-range condos.

On the upside, at least for me, I didn't see even a hint of security anywhere around, leaving me a fairly free stretch of movement.

Harris's place, 2349 Elm Drive, was on the ground level, facing front, of a four-unit building. Red brick with black trimming all around, my extremely-uneducated guess would put its asking price in the low six figures.

An awful lot to pay for basically four walls and air.

I pulled the Cherokee about a block up and around the corner.

In the midst of breaking and entering, even with Nichols's tacit approval, I had no desire to run into either Marcus or the state cops.

Walking back to Harris's condo, about half a block out I noticed

a red Camry parked in the driveway of his next-door neighbor. I
didn't stop, just slowed down my walk while doing a quick three
sixty of the neighborhood. Just like on my first drive through,
nothing looked out of place, and there was nothing in and of itself
suspicious about the red car.

Except it didn't feel right.

Duke Prowder was the veteran, grizzled private eye out of St.
Louis who took me under his wing when my wrestling career
ended. Coming up on forty and never having had a normal job or
career, I was a bit of a loss as to how to earn a living once my knee
would no longer support me in the ring.

With my only real attributes or talents being my size and the
ability to make ferocious faces, I picked up work where I could as a
part-time bouncer in various clubs around the St. Louis area, both
on the Missouri and Illinois sides of the line.

One night, Duke happened to be in a bar I was working and
spotted me handling a minor altercation. No big deal, nothing that
didn't happen at least a couple of times a week, but for some reason
I caught Duke's eye, and he offered to take me on as his assistant.

A couple of years later, after having accumulated enough hours
to qualify for my own P.I. license, I was ready to set out on my own.

In those two years, Duke taught me as much as he could, one
lesson being to pay attention to what he called the "shivers," that
vague unease you get when a situation just doesn't seem right, even
though you can't really tell why.

"I'm sure there's some fancy, psychological explanation for it,"
Duke told me one day. "Kind of like all those theories people have
as to what déjà vu actually is. Why it happens doesn't matter. All
you need to know is that when you feel the shivers, goddammit pay
attention to them."

I was getting the shivers now as I approached Harris's place.
Didn't know if it was that car parked next door, when all the other
driveways around were empty, that caused them, but whatever I
went as carefully as I could.

There was yellow crime scene tape, understandable since the
murder had taken place less than forty-eight hours ago, stretched

across Harris's door, along with a special lock the police had left there to make sure it stayed sealed.

I pulled out of my jeans pocket a small, leather pouch, another gift of Duke Prowder's, and a few minutes later I was inside.

As soon as I crossed the threshold I knew I wasn't alone.

I stopped just inside, after shutting the door (didn't want an errant neighbor walking by and wondering why a dead man's door stood open), and strained my ears as hard as I could.

I gave it about thirty seconds of not hearing anything other than total silence. I knew someone else was somewhere in there, whether aware of me or not I wasn't sure.

I put myself in the head of an intruder, not that hard since I was one myself, to figure out where they'd be lurking. About three possible choices came to me, and I went with the most obvious and set out in search of the man's bedroom.

The condo was two stories tall, which made it kind of obvious that the master bedroom would be on the second floor. A row of wooden stairs, adorned with a gray metal railing, led upwards, and I moved up as silently as I could.

A central hallway traversed the second floor, with two doors to the right and three to the left. I stopped again, at the top of the stairs, to listen, and this time my effort was rewarded.

From the first room on the right came a slight scraping sound. I eased my way there, glanced in the partially open door and saw a female form, dressed in blue jeans and a red tee-shirt, kneeling down and going through the drawers of a cherrywood dresser against the far wall.

Leaning against the door jamb and crossing my arms across my chest, I watched the woman go about her business.

She was tossing through the middle of five drawers. I wasn't sure if she'd started at the top or the bottom, though considering that nothing lay on the floor around her, and that she didn't seem to have any purse or bag with her, she clearly hadn't found anything yet.

The question was, what was she looking for?

She finished with the middle drawer and reared back on her heels, shoulders slumping in frustration.

"What happened to your 'Vette?" I asked.

The woman whirled around. At the same time, she backed against the dresser and held her hands out in front of her as if to ward off a physical attack.

In the next instant, she relaxed a little, though not much.

"Oh, it's you," Karyn Roberts said. "What are you doing here?"

Not a bad question, I thought.

Almost as good as mine.

"Back at you, Karyn. What's a retired journalist doing rummaging in a dead man's house?"

CHAPTER THIRTY-FOUR

"**I**T SEEMED LIKE A LOGICAL PLACE to start," she told me about fifteen minutes later.

We were sitting at a table in a Burger King about two miles from Harris's condo. After my abrupt appearance, I'd considered going ahead with the search as planned, holding Karyn in place by one hand if I had to.

Because I had no clue how long she'd been in the condo, and her showing up there suggested that she could possibly pose a more abundant source of knowledge about the case than anything I could find among Harris's effects.

I could always go back later, or just wait for the cops Nichols was going to send to do their thing and see what they turned up.

"A logical place to start what?" I asked as she took a drink from her Coke. I'd ordered large Cokes for both of us. Neither one of us had ordered food, but we had to look as if we had some excuse for sitting there.

"To start unraveling the mystery," she replied. "Isn't that why you were there as well?"

"Depends. What mystery are you working on?"

"The mystery of how everyone could have been so wrong twenty-five years ago."

I took a large drink from my cup, then leaned back in the booth.

"Who says they were wrong? I haven't seen or heard anything that says the original conviction was in error."

"Let's just say I have a strong investment in Sheila's innocence."

I gave her a long, hard look. Then the little bulb clicked in my head.

"You're a PR person now, right?"

Karyn smiled. "Most of the time."

"And I'm going to go out on a limb and guess that the rest of the time you're somehow associated with Amendment V."

"Actually, I'm on the board, but I try to keep that kind of quiet."

"Kansas City business bigwigs wouldn't approve?"

"Something like that."

"Tell me about this big feeling of yours," I said.

Karyn began absent-mindedly tracing circles on the table with her finger.

"You weren't living here back then, were you?"

I shook my head. "I was in St. Louis at the time. I heard about the case. It's all my mom would talk about for a while."

"It's all anyone was talking about, mainly because it was right out of a cheap soap opera. White trash girl meets and marries rich high society dude, then offs him? What self-respecting crime reporter could ask for more?"

"You weren't doing the city crime beat back then, right?"

Another nod. "Like I told you last night, the city editor at the time passed over a couple of more experienced guys to give me the shot."

"And you never gave a thought as to why?"

She took a long swallow, probably giving herself time to form an acceptable answer compared to the one the other evening.

"Of course, I did," she said, putting the cup down. "I figured there was bad blood, pardon the pun, and left it at that. Then I went out and did my job."

"And a couple of weeks later Sheila Hampton's off to prison for life."

"Until Amendment V started digging around in the transcripts and found all those shortcomings."

"And I'm guessing you were one of the ones who instigated them taking her on."

"Instigated?" She gave a short, barking laugh. "I insisted. The damned case had been bugging me for years. I finally reached the point where I had the ability to do something about it."

It was my turn now to drink and contemplate. I looked around at the nearly empty, mid-day restaurant. The few customers in the place, mainly teenagers skipping school, were totally ignoring the middle-aged couple sitting in a booth discussing murder and conspiracy.

"Why?" I asked.

"Why what?"

"Why did it suddenly become such a crusade for you after all this time?"

"Isn't a possible injustice reason enough? I'm sure that's what your friend Mr. Lyman would say."

"My friend Mr. Lyman may have a bit of a blind spot in regards to all this."

"But you're more pragmatic?" she asked.

"I'm not exactly a world-renowned investigator or anything, but I'm able to look at the thing head on, without any sort of emotional investment."

"And determine what?" She peered at me, seemingly genuinely interested in what I thought.

"The simplest, most logical reading is that the original investigators had it right. I haven't yet seen or heard anything that suggests other than Sheila murdered her husband and wasn't smart enough to do it right."

Karyn leaned back in her side of the booth. "What if there were an informant that said different?" she asked. "Someone involved back then who thought differently?"

"I'm guessing it was this informant that came to you and gave you a way to rectify your old feelings."

"Rectify's kind of a fancy word for an ex-jock," she said.

"Don't change the subject. Who contacted you?"

She did a few more finger tracings on the table, then looked up. "It was Harris."

"Excuse me?"

"Robert Harris. He called us out of the blue, told us he had an original copy of the trial transcript and wanted to point out some irregularities. We made an appointment, he drove out and laid it out for us. Said he knew for a fact that Sheila had gotten a bum steer and wanted to set it right."

"He thought she was innocent?" I asked.

Karyn paused and thought that one over. "I'm not sure about that. Through the four or five times we talked with him, he was kind of ambivalent at that idea."

"Like it didn't matter?"

"More or less. He didn't want her set free as much as getting a new trial."

I leaned back to mull that one over. A group of teenagers, three boys and two girls, stood up from a booth on the other side of the room and headed our way. I instinctively tensed, even though they didn't look like hoods.

More like five kids who couldn't stand the thought of school while it was warm outside.

The guy in front, who looked big and burly enough to be wearing a letter jacket as soon as fall came along, stopped at our table.

"Excuse me, sir."

"Yeah," I said, keeping an eye on him while surreptitiously glancing around the rest of the room. For all I knew, old Marcus and the Hamptons had an auxiliary delinquent corp.

"I'm sorry to bother you, but aren't you the Blond Bomber?"

Out of the corner of my eye, Karyn rolled her eyes.

No doubt thought I'd paid the kids off to come over and impress her.

"I used to be, back in my performing days," I said.

The kid turned to his friends. The two other boys, both a couple of inches shorter and about thirty pounds lighter than their leader, looked slightly agog, while the girls acted bored by it all. The lead kid turned back to me.

"I thought so. My old man used to take me to matches and I'd sometimes see you."

Karyn sighed.

"Always nice to meet a fan," I said, half expecting him to ask me for an autograph.

The kid answered. "Actually, my old man was more into you. I always kind of liked the Turbaned Tiger."

"Come on, Joey," one of the girls said. "I want to go."

"Sure thing." The kid took a step back. "Be seeing you, mister. I figured if I tell my dad I met you he'll get off my back about my homework for a while."

As the five of them headed off, Karyn snickered.

"Fame is fleeting," I said.

"Sure, big fellow. Now how about we get back to the real world, huh?"

I composed myself, too tough to cry in embarrassment.

"You're honestly telling me that the same prosecutor who sent Sheila away was the person who worked to get her sprung?"

"That's what I'm saying."

"Then what were you looking for at his house?" I asked.

A shifty look came into her eyes.

"Hand it over," I said, putting as much steel as possible into my tone.

"What?"

"Whatever you took from his place before I showed up. We're both working for the same thing, so why bother holding out?"

"What does it matter?" Karyn asked. "All I have to do is make sure whatever I find goes to the right . . ."

"It matters because there are some bad people floating around this thing, some dangerous people, and you may not be up to the task of fending them off. Or didn't last night teach you anything?"

Karyn scrunched her face for a second, then reached into her pocket and pulled out a sliver of metal. Sliding it across the table to me, I saw that it was a safety deposit box key.

Picking the key up, I saw only the number 23 on it. No other identifying marks. Providence is a small city, true. But it's not that small. Going through every bank in town, not to mention the surrounding county area, would take a week at least.

"Where'd you find it?" I asked.

"Hiding in plain sight, as it were. It was in the backing behind a picture of his wife."

"How'd you find that?"

She shrugged. "Seemed the obvious place to look, especially if you consider she died last year."

I frowned, my brain feeling sluggish. It took me a minute to put two and two together.

"You saying it was his wife dying that made him decide to come forward to you guys?"

"If you look at the timing, it seems possible. If, and I stress if, he was involved in railroading Sheila . . ."

"Then he was keeping quiet while she was alive. Now he feels unburdened."

"Would be my guess."

Something about that scenario didn't sound quite right, but at the moment I couldn't find the glitch.

"I don't suppose you happen to know what bank, do you?" I asked.

"No. When he first contacted us, Harris gave us an affidavit with the basic information, the points in the trial where either he or Judge Jackson had short-circuited the process."

"All very legally, I'm guessing."

"Oh, very much so. Then, a few weeks ago, after we already had the ball rolling, he e-mailed us that he had certain information secured in a bank, and that once she was out he would turn it over to us. Of course, before he could he was killed."

I whirled the key back and forth in my fingers. "Kind of old-fashioned, though, isn't it? I mean, it's like something out of the seventies. Whatever happened to computer files, thumb drives or the cloud?"

Karyn grinned and finished off her drink. "Maybe he figured that with everyone knowing the new-fangled stuff going old school would be better."

"Maybe."

"Or maybe he was an old enough duffer that this just came natural to him."

"You may want to reconsider the old stuff," I said. "When he died, Harris didn't have that many years on either you or me."

Shaking her head, Karyn snatched the key back from me. "Either way, doesn't help us to narrow it down. What good's his evidence if . . ." She paused, a look of near horror coming over her face.

"What is it?" I asked.

"I just realized, what if this is what got him killed? Someone must have figured out he was our source, but how?"

I was kind of surprised she hadn't thought of that already and felt it would be kind of petty to bring it up. Plus, I could think of only one way to go at it.

"The way I see it," I said, "there's no way any one person could have railroaded Sheila so effectively. The judge, the prosecutor, the cops investigating. When you look everything over, none of them are too far out of line."

"That's pretty much the impression he gave us. But if you put them all together . . ." she said.

"If you put them all together," I began, then trailed off.

"What is it?" she asked after a minute of me staring off into space.

I said, speaking slowly to allow my thoughts to catch up, "There's a chance it wouldn't be enough. Whoever framed her, and I have a pretty good idea who that was, would want to make sure they left absolutely nothing to chance. They needed an absolute slam dunk, and for that, there's one crucial piece of the puzzle they'd have to use."

Karyn's face paled, and I figured that she'd just put two and two together herself.

"No way. You don't mean . . ."

I felt sick to my stomach as I did so. "If you're going to go to this much trouble to frame someone, why not pull out all the stops? What if Howard Landon, her defense attorney, was in on it?"

"How do you go about finding out?" Karyn asked.

"I'm guessing that's what Harris was trying to do. We have to find that box."

"How did you come to be at his house?"

"I was going on the backtrack method. Tracking down all the major participants in the original trial, seeing what they would tell me about it."

"You think she's innocent of Derek's killing as well?" Karyn asked.

"Honestly, I don't know. If I had to take a stand, I'd say no. She probably did it. But looking at it that way doesn't give me anywhere to go except that she's guilty this time as well. And since the cops are already pretty much pursuing that angle, I figured someone should look at it the other way."

Karyn smiled, and her eyes honest to goodness crinkled for a moment.

"What?" I asked.

"You're an old-fashioned type guy. You're trying to bluff through it, but it's not working. You're all for truth, justice and the American Way."

I growled in my throat, her near flattery making me uncomfortable. "Hardly. I'm just a guy who's angling for some free legal work down the line. Bernie wouldn't like it much if I ended up proving his client guilty."

"Uh huh," she said. "So what now?"

I'd been thinking about that and I didn't like what I'd come up with.

"I think we need to divide forces for a while. Do you have some associates close by who can help you check out banks?"

"Not really. Most of our people are located around either our KC or St. Louis chapters."

"Even with the state capitol close by?"

She laughed, softly, and I realized I liked her laugh almost as much as her crinkling eyes. "We're not exactly a national organization, Quinton. Plus, there's something you may have overlooked."

"Which is?"

"You actually think any bank's going to let me just walk right in and ask if it's their key? And even if they did, wouldn't that raise a whole lot of questions as to how I happened to have a dead man's box key?"

I felt like kicking myself but figured I'd bruise myself if I did so.

"That's a point," I said, trying to make it sound like no big deal. "Any suggestions?"

"Why don't I get some of our people on to it and see if there's some legal way to get at his box?"

"Wouldn't any briefs you prepare have to presuppose knowledge of the box? How would you explain that?"

"We could bury it in some sort of generalized paperwork. Even if we get turned down, we may get the name of the bank, and from there we could figure something out."

"Okay," I said, "go ahead and give it a shot. Move very slowly and carefully. If this is as big as it seems, we don't know who all has been corrupted in this thing."

Karyn laughed, although there was a strained quality to it. "Are there any cops you trust?"

I stood up and grabbed both her cup and mine to take them to the trash basket.

"One or two," I said. "I'm just not sure I trust the people above them."

"What are you going to do?" she asked.

"What I should have done from the start," I said. "Begin low and work my way up."

CHAPTER THIRTY-FIVE

I PULLED UP TO MIKE PALMER'S HOUSE a little before six, cut the engine and sat motionless for a few minutes, checking out the lay of the land. Didn't see any gremlins hanging around, let alone dark blue Lincolns. I departed the vehicle, walked up the walkway and rang the doorbell.

Because his garage door was shut, I couldn't tell offhand if the ex-cop was home or not. A second or two after I rang, I heard a shuffling on the other side of the door.

The peephole darkened for the merest flicker of an instant, them Palmer's voice, a little more ragged than the other day, spoke up.

Which could have just been because he was talking through the door.

Uh huh.

"What do you want?"

I frowned, both wondering and fearing why he hadn't opened up. "Wanted to talk to you, Mike."

"What about?"

Through the closed door, and by now my nerves were starting to jangle. "What say you open up and we can do this normal-like?"

Another long pause. "Go away, Quinton. Got nothing to say to you."

"Maybe so," I said, "but I need some pointers, and I think you can supply them."

"I'm not a cop anymore, so beat it."

"Mike, open the goddamned door before I break it in."

I waited, giving him the time to either raise or fold.

"You just try it, Quinton, and I'll put you down sure as you're breathing."

"The way you put Marcus and his boys down when they showed up?"

Sometimes a shot in the dark is better than no shot at all.

I waited again, counting down the seconds. Made it to twenty before the sound of a chain rattling.

When Palmer opened the door, my first question was how many rounds had he gone through with those guys.

The ex-cop's face was completely mottled, blacks and blues fighting with each other for dominance. One eye was swollen nearly shut, and there were rough scrapes running up and down both of his hands.

He was wearing blue jeans and a long-sleeved white shirt, and I could only wonder what the rest of his torso looked like.

"Don't know anyone named Marcus," he said. "Other than that you've got the basic idea."

Although I'd come over there intending to raise hell with the man, seeing him ambulatory with those kinds of wounds raised my respect for him about a zillion notches. Since he'd started on the force young and retired relatively early, he was about a decade older than me, and I couldn't help but wonder if I could take that much of a beating and remain breathing, let alone upright.

"What'd they want?" I asked, as if I didn't know.

The old cop grimaced, whether through mental or physical pain I wasn't sure, and stepped out on the porch. Motioning me toward the closed garage, he said, "You think what they did to me is bad, come look at this."

He flicked a switch on the outside of the garage, and the door began creaking and whining its way up. As it reached about the halfway point, I could see what Palmer had referred to.

The old antique Harley, that had looked about halfway restored on my previous visit, lay in about eighty pieces on the garage floor.

I've never been a bike man myself, but I could at least somewhat empathize with the man's pain.

"You have any kids, Quinton?" he asked, his voice raspy and pained.

"No," I said, "married once, a long time ago, but nothing came of it."

"Wife died about eight years ago, thyroid cancer. Since then, bikes have been my kids. Buy them, refurbish them, then find them a good home. This was the sixth one I've been working on. Look at it now."

"What was their message?" I asked.

"What do you think? Don't talk about Derek or Sheila Hampton, say nothing to anyone about that night."

"You call the cops?" I asked, sounding like an idiot even as I asked it.

"What are you, an idiot? Haven't you figured out yet how far these people's reach extends?"

I shook my head, not sure what to say to that.

"Fuck it," Palmer said a moment later. "Come on in the house and I'll get us some coffee."

"Coffee?" A few minutes ago the man wouldn't even open the door to me.

"Yeah," he said, looking down at the pile of scrap metal in front of us. "Coffee and a talk. After all these years of staying quiet, I've had just about enough of those two."

CHAPTER THIRTY-SIX

I STAYED AT PALMER'S FOR ABOUT HALF AN HOUR, talking a little bit but mainly listening as the retired cop and I sat at the table in his small dining alcove. Although he'd made the coffee, after a sip or two both of us forgot it as Palmer laid out his tale for me. It was composed of part facts, part speculation, and while the speculation dwarfed the facts, I'd developed enough respect for the old street cop to place my faith in his words.

Leaving his house, I stopped outside the Cherokee and placed a call to Bernie's office. I didn't have anything I wanted to report yet, not until I had a whole lot more facts to back me up, but figured I owed him a check in. I wasn't sure if he'd be there this late in the evening although sometimes I thought the guy worked the same twenty hours a day as he had back when he'd been a first-year associate. He wasn't there, but one of his associates informed me that he was in court on an arraignment hearing, and they expected him back within the hour.

"An arraignment at this hour?" I asked and was informed that one of their long-time clients had been picked up just that day, on what the young lawyer wouldn't tell me, and was demanding to be either charged immediately or let go.

I left a message for Bernie to get ahold of me ASAP, then climbed behind the wheel and pondered my next move.

There were two ways I could go: the smart way and the dumb way. My instincts were shrieking at me to go dumb. I barely knew

Sheila Hampton, had only spent the briefest of times with her, and
to be honest didn't care for her that much. My impression, granted
colored by her quarter century in the pen, was that she was pretty
much as she'd been depicted in the press back then, an old-fashioned gold digger who married Derek Hampton, not for love or
even affection, but for the easy life he represented.

Then again, who was I to criticize? Back in my wrestling days,
I had my fair share of groupies, before, during and after my marriage to Pamela. Odds were that the majority of them were only
interested in a couple of things, money being item number one.
The guys and I used to always locker-room joke about how dumb
those girls had to be.

Except for the six months that I wrestled in the big leagues,
my average salary usually equaled what a good warehouse stocker
would make. My best time, of course, was when I was champion.
Even then, considering I worked for the Midwest Wrestling League,
my actual pay didn't amount to all that much.

So yeah, who was I to look down on Sheila Hampton?

I sat in my car for a few minutes, drumming my fingers on the
steering wheel, before firing up the ignition.

Maybe I was getting old, or was my experience being caught
in the middle of a Mafia war earlier in the year tarnishing me? I
changed my mind and decided to at least give the smart way a shot.

And if that didn't work, I could always fall back on the dumb way.

JOSH NICHOLS WAS AT HIS DESK, situated close to his new lieutenant's closed office, scowling at about three inches of paperwork in
front of him. When he saw me, his scowl deepened.

"You guys should get a computer," I said as I dropped into the
single tubular chair facing his desk. "Save you a lot of time and
hassle."

"Very funny," Nichols replied. "What do you want?"

For the first time, I noticed a couple of lines in my buddy's face.
That, plus a few traces of gray in his otherwise brown hair gave me
a bit of an idea of the tension he'd been under lately. At thirty-two,
Nichols was young enough he shouldn't have those marks.

I thought about bandying around a bit with Josh, seeing how far I could push his temper, but decided to take it easy on him. Things hadn't exactly been smooth between us lately.

"Sheila Hampton," I said.

"Don't even start, Blondie. She was damned lucky to get let out the first time around. Only an idiot would turn right around and land back in dutch again."

"She wasn't lucky to get out, Josh. There were reversible grounds. Truth is, I'm starting to think that you people were played like fools the first time around."

"What do you mean, you people? I was in grade school at the time."

"You know what I mean."

Nichols slumped in his chair and glared at me.

"What's your point, Sam?"

I looked around to make sure no one was close by. Truthfully, getting on toward eight o'clock the squad room was almost deserted.

"You looking for something?" Nichols said.

"Prying ears and eyes, guy. I just came from Mike Palmer's place."

"How's old Mike doing?"

"Not too good lately. Especially since he decided to grow a conscience."

"Huh?"

"Palmer was the first OOS when Derek Hampton was murdered."

Nichols's eyes crossed for a minute. "Okay?"

"A few guys visited him this afternoon. They wanted to make sure he'd stay in line."

"Come again? Stay in line for what?"

"The official story of the Hampton killing is a web of lies, Josh. And Palmer was one of the spinners."

"One of the . . ."

"You know a guy named Leslie Brown?"

"Detective Brown? Sure. He's been a member of this department for . . ."

"For almost thirty years," I broke in. I pulled out of my pocket a small spiral notebook and flicked it open. Almost made me feel like a real detective. "Joined the Providence force at age twenty-four. Made a big splash for himself a couple of times, then promoted to detective at the age of thirty-one. Right?"

"I don't have his personnel file memorized. Sounds about right."

"Uh huh." I glanced over the notes again. "And ever since then he's been at the same rank, same station. A couple of lateral moves in terms of assignments, but he didn't even make it to sergeant in all that time." I flicked my gaze at Nichols. "How long did it take for you to make sergeant, Josh?"

He stared at me, and I could almost see things clicking in his head.

"His most notable career highlight," I continued, "was being the lead investigator on the Derek Hampton murder. According to several of the jurors afterwards, his testimony about his interrogations with Sheila was some of the most persuasive evidence presented at the trial."

"The point being?"

I flicked a couple of pages in the book, more for effect than anything else. I actually had most of the information memorized.

"Robert Harris, hot shot prosecutor with bright political future. Successfully prosecuted the Hampton trial and shortly after was being talked about as a possible future DA, if not state legislator."

"Sam . . ."

I held up my hand and continued. "Judge Lois Jackson. We all know that one, right? Superior court judge here in Carson County, solid record, minimal times overturned on appeal."

"So?" Nichols asked, though his tone showed his increasing interest.

"Yet in all these years not even one rung up on the ladder? Back in the early 2,000's she was being talked about, often, as a possible state supreme court judge, if not even higher. One or two speculations over the years on why she didn't get appointed to a couple of federal bench openings. She checks off all the boxes, but for some reason neither of our state senators ever recommended her. And she sat in limbo."

Nichols stared at me, softly tapping his fingers on his desk. "Okay, sounds like there's a pattern there."

"A pattern that broke last year when Charlotte Harris passed away from bone cancer."

My cop buddy leaned back in his chair, his face losing a little color. "I hadn't heard about that. He's been retired for a while, and I never knew him that well anyway."

"What do you think of it? His wife passes away. And, believe it or not, before long he starts contacting Amendment V about problems with the Hampton trial. Be a stretch to call it a coincidence, but add it on to him being gunned down right after she's out of prison, and what do you have?" I asked.

"Are you for real? You're talking conspiracy, Blondie. You're saying that Sheila's original trial . . ."

"Was tainted," I finished for him, "from start to finish. Now you tell me, Det. Sergeant Nichols, who would have had the most to gain, two decades ago, from Derek Hampton's death?"

"The other two, of course," Josh said.

"That's right. Put Derek down, get Sheila out of the way, and they've got all that money. Not to mention control of the family company back. Sounds like a motive to me."

Josh shook his head. "Doesn't make sense, buddy. Let's say they wanted to get their baby brother out of the way, along with Sheila. Why not just kill them both and be done with it?"

"Yeah," I said, "that part bothered me for a while, too. Then I gave it a little more thought. If both Derek and Sheila had ended up dead, who would the obvious suspects be."

"Christ," Josh said as he rubbed his hand across his face. "We'd look at whoever had the strongest motive."

"Which would have been?"

"Jesus Christ," he repeated. "You telling me those two old rich people are that damned devious?"

"Makes sense if you think about it. Kill both of them, George and Mary become obvious suspects. Maybe not top of the list, but awful close. But kill Derek and offer her up on a platter . . ."

"And the whole thing's tied up into a neat bundle."

"Pretty much."

Josh leaned forward, his face turning red. I didn't know if he was angry with me or with what may have been done to our local justice system.

"You realize this is all speculation," he said.

I nodded.

"I can't do anything with just speculation."

"Could you at least keep Harris's case open, continue the investigation?"

"Based on what? In case you've forgotten, guy, the murder weapon had your client's fingerprints on it."

"Actually, she's Bernie's client."

"Don't play semantics with me, Sam. The weapon had her prints; she has no alibi; and you can't deny she's got one hell of a motive. I don't have anything to use as a basis to keep investigating."

"You going to tell me the fact the print report came back so fast doesn't bother you? Or that the whole damned thing just seems a bit too pat and easy?"

"I'd say that's Lyman's job."

I gave my buddy the most conciliatory look I could.

"What if I got you something?" I asked.

"Hell," he grinned for the first time since I'd shown up, "I thought you'd never offer."

CHAPTER THIRTY-SEVEN

B Y THE TIME I LEFT THE STATION, it was getting on to nine o'clock, and my stomach reminded me it had been hours since I'd eaten. I thought about heading home for a bite, shower and bed, but as I headed down the sidewalk to the parking garage where I'd left the Cherokee the mingled aromas from my favorite Providence BBQ joint came wafting my way.

I paused, considered my options, then pulled out my phone and made a call.

"Hello?" Karyn Roberts answered on the third ring.

"Hello yourself. How's your evening going?"

She paused for a moment. "Is this Quinton?"

"Yep, the Blond Bomber himself. Have you eaten yet?"

"Of course, I have. The night's half over."

"True," I said, "but I haven't, and I'm standing half a block from the best BBQ in the state of Missouri."

She laughed in my ear. "You're kidding, right? You forgetting that I live in KC? You honestly think you can beat us when it comes to BBQ?"

"The people who own the place I'm standing in front of think KC's overrated."

"Maybe so," Karyn said. "I'd say it's academic anyway, seeing as I've already eaten."

"Yeah," I said. "How'd you end up with the banks?"

"Give us time, Quinton. By the time I got hold of someone and explained the situation, it was too late in the day to get started. We're going to go on the assumption that he used an institution close to where he lived and move on from there."

"Not bad," I said as I opened up the restaurant's door and held it for a young couple going out. They were in early twenties and were almost wearing signs that proclaimed them university students. "Though if he was worried about someone pegging to what he was doing he may have gone far afield, make it harder to track."

"Maybe," she sounded rather doubtful, "but we're going with percentages. A couple of our sharper brains are trying to come up with a legal way to track down and get into his box. You want me to give you a call when they come up with something?"

I thought about my talk with Mike Palmer, and of how tangled this whole thing appeared. Out of the blue, I began to feel a little concerned.

"You still at your friend's house?" I asked.

"No. After what happened last night, I figured it was better to get a hotel room. Didn't want to put my buddy in harm's way."

I frowned a bit at the word "buddy." That tag usually implied a male, and I began to have unsettling thoughts about just how close this "friend" of hers was.

Then I chided myself on being such a flake. Hip-deep in a murder investigation was no time to get all crushy over a woman I'd just met.

"Last chance on dinner," I said. "There's only one person in line ahead of me, but I can wait until you get here."

She laughed, and I felt myself breathing again. "Try me another night, Quinton. Honestly, I'd love to, but I'm about tuckered out from the last few days. Think I'm going to take a dip in the hotel's jacuzzi and call it a day."

I growled deep in my throat to hide my disappointment. "Okay," I said. "Call you tomorrow and touch base."

"Do that, and thanks for the invite."

She hung up her phone, and I put mine back in my pocket.

"Kansas City BBQ sucks," I said to the guy in front of me.

CHAPTER THIRTY-EIGHT

T HE NEXT MORNING, A LITTLE AFTER NINE, I tracked Leslie Brown down at a ballpark a few blocks from his house. Odd for him to be doing batting practice at such a time, but detectives keep odd hours. I stood a ways off from the batting cage to scope the guy out. Brown and I had run into each other a couple of times over the years. We weren't friends or anything, though as far as I knew we weren't enemies either.

I had a feeling that was about to change.

He was early fifties, which would have made him practically a brand-new detective at the time of the original trial. This put him a bit older than my forty-six, though not all that much. It's amazing how, the older I get the less the spans between years seem to matter.

Brown stood six two with a rather lanky build. As I watched him, I had the feeling of his body being hollowed out, as if a once muscular build had atrophied from the inside out. Washed out brown eyes and straggly brownish-gray hair completed the rather dejected look of the detective.

A much younger man, no more than thirty and with a linebacker's build, was throwing a variety of pitches his way, and to his credit for the few minutes I observed Brown hit more than he missed. After the tenth or twelfth pitch popped out into the infield, he turned and looked right at me.

"Something I can do for you?"

"Sorry to bother you, Detective. I don't know if you remember me . . ."

"You kidding, Quinton? Who could forget a guy like you? Especially when you're working for a killer."

"Nice to see that good old presumption of innocence is alive and well. But seeing as I do have a job to do, you mind giving me a couple of minutes?"

For a second or two he didn't move, just stood there in a half stance, bat slung across his shoulder. Then he waved off the young pitcher, who walked over to the far stands, where he began gulping a bottle of Gatorade.

I fondly remembered the days when my gut was that strong.

"What the hell?" Brown said. "Always time for an old guy like you."

I thought about pointing out I was over five years younger than he was before deciding to take the high road. I also made a note to doublecheck my hair the next time I was in front of a mirror. Maybe more of the gray had been mixing into the blond lately than I'd realized.

Or maybe it was finally time to cut my hair and start looking more like a grownup than a punk rocker'.

Brown walked over to a portion of the stands where he had his gear resting and, without letting go of his bat, bent down to grab a towel to begin wiping the sweat off his face. I followed him.

"What is it you want to know?" he asked with his back still to me. "I'm not on the case this time around."

"You were the first time," I pointed out.

He paused, half crouched over, then dropped the towel into his duffel bag and stood up straight. He turned to face me.

"Yeah, I was. My first major squeal as a primary. What's your point?"

"Pretty big case for you."

He shrugged. "Pretty good case for everyone."

"Yeah, but according to most of the media analysts it was your testimony that put her away."

He started to turn away from me.

"Been a real boost to your career since then, huh Brown?"

The cop froze, his shoulders tensing under his tee shirt. He flicked a glance towards the young guy sitting on the far bleachers waiting for us to finish up.

"Whadda you mean, Quinton?"

He had his back to me, and I was keeping an eye on his right hand, the one that hadn't let go of the bat. "Just seems odd to me. You were fairly young, only a few months since promotion, had this big bust and moment in the limelight, and all these years later you're right where you were."

Brown didn't reply. If anything the tension in his body seemed to intensify.

I decided to hammer it home a little, see if I could get a reaction, yet at the same time I set myself in case that reaction became violent.

"Looks to me like you've been under someone's thumb the whole time. At least Harris was man enough to eventually fight back."

"Shit!" the word exploded out of him. "You categorize Robert Harris as a man? That turd couldn't win a trial if his life depended on it, not without someone helping him out every step of the way."

"He won the Hampton trial."

Now Brown turned fully to me, and I wasn't quite sure what I saw in his eyes.

"Like I said, he can win anything as long as he has the help. If he's on his own . . ."

"And you were part of the help on the Hampton case," I said, not as a question.

"Part of it?" He took the bat off his shoulder and did a light practice swing. He swiveled his hips to do so, and the bat didn't come anywhere near me, but I set myself a little deeper all the same. "I was practically his whole case. Sewed it up and brought it in for the home team."

"And didn't get rewarded."

Brown had begun another practice swing, and he halted in mid swing, his knuckles whitening on the handle. "Be careful there, buddy. You may be playing with more fire than you can handle."

I hung my arms loose at my sides, my fingers half curled. "What else am I supposed to think, Leslie? I got news for you. It's starting to come undone. May want to get out in front of it."

His shoulders tensed more, and those fingers of his were damned near melded into the bat handle. He glanced to the side to where his pitcher sat waiting for us. From his distance, I doubted that the guy could see what was going down.

"Bullshit," Brown said. "You're just blowing smoke. Your client's guilty. She managed to slither out once, but it's not going to happen again."

"She had no motive to go after Harris."

Brown barked out a laugh and lowered the bat.

I didn't lower my guard.

"What are you talking about? No motive? She was out to get the guy who put her away. What the hell kind of detective are you, Quinton?"

"He was also the guy who sprung her," I said.

Brown's face screwed up into about twenty different combinations of confusion. "Come again?"

"It was Harris who first contacted the Amendment V people. He's the one who sicced them on to Sheila's cause."

Although the bat dropped out of his hands, I didn't relax. In my periphery, I saw Brown's partner beginning to shift back and forth a bit.

"That bastard," the detective said in a half whisper. "He's going to get us all killed."

Okay, I'd expected a reaction but not quite that one reaction.

Now what the hell could I do with it?

As it turned out, I wasn't going to have time to think out my next move because as I started to answer my phone rang.

I pulled it out of my pocket, glanced at the screen.

"Yeah?" I said, hoping the caller would get the point from my gruff tone.

"Blondie," Josh Nichols said, "where are you right now?"

I glanced at Brown. "Talking things over with an old acquaintance. What's up, guy?"

With no clear idea of where Brown stood, the last thing I wanted was to let him know his sergeant was on the other end.

"Why don't you drop what you're doing and get over to Mike Palmer's house?"

"Why?" I asked. "I was just there last night and . . ."

"Sam," Nichols's tone dropped a couple of levels, "best get over here right now."

Oh, yeah. I could tell from the frostiness in my buddy's voice that Brown had called it right.

From his grave, Harris was getting them all killed.

CHAPTER THIRTY-NINE

IT WAS GETTING TO BE A PATTERN, and one I didn't care a whole lot for. Lately, almost every time I met up with Nichols was at a crime scene.

Just like the last time, I wheeled the Cherokee into Palmer's street. I had to stop about a block away from his house, the whole darned area cordoned off by patrol cars, blue and reds strobing in the bright sunlight, and one lone ambulance parked about fifty feet from Palmer's driveway, the attendants nowhere in sight.

I climbed out of my car and headed toward the first of three cordons surrounding the scene. In the middle of the morning, with most people at work or school, there shouldn't have been many bystanders. But the old cop's neighborhood must have had more than its share of retirees or night workers because I had to wend my way through a throng of gawkers.

One or two gave me odd looks, no doubt wondering, with my burly build, jeans, tee-shirt and long hair why I wasn't in police custody myself.

Sometimes, I kind of wondered the same thing.

The officer manning the barricades, a young Latino guy who'd frequented my gym for the last year or so, smiled when I approached and at my short, "Nichols sent for me," waved me on through.

One of the nice things about Providence being such a small city is that you spend time with one or two cops and before long you know most of them on the force. A few nods of the heads to another uniform or two, and before I knew it I was inside the house, keeping just inside the door so I wouldn't muck up the scene, and looking down at Mike Palmer.

Nichols and two other detectives, an older man wearing a rumpled gray suit and a pretty young Latina in navy slacks and tan jacket, were standing off to the side of the corpse. I edged my way around to avoid disturbing any possible evidence and joined them. Nichols glanced at me before returning his attention to Palmer's corpse.

"How'd you find him?" I asked.

Nichols shook his head. "After you left the office last night, I started wondering. First thing this morning I sent these two," he pointed to the other detectives, "to check things out. They found him and called us in."

The retired cop was lying on his right side, eyes fixed toward the kitchen doorway, with half his head blown off. He was wearing the same clothes he'd had on when I'd spoken to him earlier. There wasn't any upset furniture or any other signs of a struggle, and I couldn't see a weapon anywhere around.

"Big gun," I said, remembering the .45 that Marcus, the Hamptons' security dude, wore.

"Brilliant deduction," the Hispanic detective said.

"Sorry, April. It's the best I can do."

April Clemente shook her head and turned away from me. Nichols caught my eye and motioned me outside.

Stepping out onto the porch, I took a deep breath. "Looks pretty straightforward," I said.

"If you say so, except for the fact that we don't know who killed him."

"Yeah," I muttered. "there is that."

"We'll have to wait to hear what the docs say. He looks pretty stiff to me, like he hasn't yet gone out of rigor. It may have happened right after you left. Think they were watching his house?'

"Could have been. I didn't see anything out of the norm, but I wasn't really looking either."

"Either way," Nichols said, "I should have gone with my hunch instead of sleeping on it."

"Don't do that to yourself, Josh. If you'd sent someone over to check him out, there's no telling they wouldn't have just waited till later."

"Maybe. At least your client's off the hook on this one. Hard to kill a guy when you're locked up downtown."

Not having anything to say to that, I stayed silent.

Nichols and I stepped aside as the medical examiner, a blond-haired guy of around thirty-five or so, hustled up the porch and into the house. Nichols watched him go in, then reached up and rubbed the back of his neck.

"Clemente is the lead on this. I'll need you to come in sometime soon and give her a statement."

I felt a faint rumbling in my gut. "You may want to keep an eye on the others," I said. "I just came from talking to Brown. If they've taken out Palmer here, who's to say they're going to stop with him."

"Dammit, Blondie, we don't even know who 'they' are."

"Yes, we do. It's George and Mary Hampton."

"You think it's the Hamptons, but you don't have any proof. I need more than the say-so of a health club owner before I take on one of the richest families in the state."

"Then I'll get you the proof," I said. "Somehow or other. In the meantime, keep an eye on Brown. Make sure someone doesn't take him out as well. And you'd better call the state troopers."

"For the judge?" Nichols asked. "I figured they were already on this. Didn't you say that one of them came by to warn you off?"

"Right, to warn me off. He thought it was a matter of simple harassment. This is obviously turning into something much bigger. They managed to pull a fast one twenty-five years ago, and they want to make sure it stays out of sight.

Nichols nodded. "I see your point."

"They may decide to go for a clean sweep, and if they do . . ." I paused, a new premonition wiggling into my mind.

"Got to go," I said and stepped off the porch. Before Nichols could respond, I was halfway out of the yard. Once past the outer cordon I bolted for my car as quick as I could go.

Of all the principal players in Sheila's trial two decades ago, only Brown and Judge Jackson were left to tell the tale. However, there was someone else who had recently become involved in the whole business, and I was scared to death for her.

CHAPTER FORTY

CLIMBING INTO THE CHEROKEE, I pulled out my phone and called Karyn's number. My heart skipped a couple of times as it rang once, then again, before she answered on the third ring.

"Hello?"

"It's me," I said without identifying myself. "Where are you?"

"In my hotel room, catching up on some paperwork."

"Related to Sheila?" I asked.

She chuckled. "Hardly. Don't forget I have a full-time day job, and at the moment I've been away from the office for a couple of days."

"Do me a favor, Karyn. Don't ask why. Just go right now and lock your door."

"Huh? It's already locked. What's the deal?"

One of those simple little things that distinguish guys from women, I thought. A man would maybe have his front door locked, maybe not, without thinking much about it. At least at night.

A woman alone would always have the door locked.

Score one for the feminine side.

"Okay, then," I said, "then do me this favor instead. I'm coming over, be there in about fifteen minutes or so. Don't open the door for anyone, okay? No one but me."

"Sam? What are you . . ."

"I'm on my way. Now, dammit promise me you won't open that door."

"Fine, if it's that important to you, I won't. But can you just tell me what is . . ."

"I think someone may be coming for you, Karyn. I think you may be in danger."

"Danger?"

By this point, I'd started my car and was pulling onto the cross street of Palmer's. In Providence you're never far from a main artery, and I pumped the Cherokee up to highway-level speed.

"I'm going to be there soon. I'll explain it all then. Just stay put."

Rather than try to converse and drive at the same time, I flung my phone down in the passenger seat and accelerated even more.

ONCE I HIT THE DOWNTOWN AREA I had to keep my speed at least within safe limits. Still, it didn't take more than ten minutes from when I'd called Karyn till I was pulling up into the parking lot of her hotel.

Fortunately, by now it was close enough to lunch time that several slots were open, and I had the Cherokee parked fairly close to the front door.

At which time I slowed myself down, turned off the ignition and took a minute to surveil the area.

From about fifty feet away, I could look through the hotel's clear glass doors and see a couple of counter clerks going about their business. A few business-looking types were walking out at the same time an older woman, amazingly wearing a black fur coat in September, entered. The two businessmen stood aside and let the old lady cross the threshold first, then they exited the hotel and climbed into a dark blue BMW and drove away.

No one was panicking, or running in fear from a gun battle. No alarms going off or hotel employees dashing back and forth.

Okay.

I grabbed my phone from the seat beside me and dialed Karyn's number again.

"What?" she answered, her tone kind of peevish.

"You in your room?" I asked.

A deep, aggrieved sigh sounded in my ear. "Yes, Quinton, I'm in my room. Now what the hell . . ."

"Stay there," I snapped. "I'll be right up."

Before leaving the car, I grabbed my gun from a door pocket and snagged a light nylon windbreaker from the back seat. Climbing out of the car, in a flash I had gun and holster snugged in the small of my back and jacket draped over me.

Then I headed towards those glass doors.

Barely three minutes later, the elevator dinged on Karyn's floor and I walked out, swiveling to scope out both ends of the hallway.

Nothing.

I began breathing a little easier.

Only a little.

Turning right, I made my way to her room and knocked on the door.

"Who is it?" she asked from the other side of the panel.

"Open the door, Karyn."

"I asked who it is."

I sighed and tried thinking of some sharp response. Before I could, the elevator door dinged open and three tough-looking young men, two tall blonds and a medium-sized redhead, all three wearing jeans, white shirts and dress jackets, marched out.

They barely paused before turning and heading in my direction.

"Forget it!" I snapped at the door. "Stay in there and call the cops."

The three men fanned out around me, their hands hovering close to the smalls of their backs.

Guess they and I went to the same handgun-concealment classes.

"You may want to move away, old man," the redhead, standing in the middle of the fan, said.

"Maybe," I replied, "then again, maybe not."

The goon didn't take his eyes off me, but the two blonds exchanged swift glances.

"The lady's calling the police right now," I said, "and any minute now someone else may come up to this floor. You might as well just turn tail and take off."

The two sidemen glanced at each other again, and this time a bit of a snicker passed between them as well.

"Here's another idea," the redhead, obviously the company spokesman, said, "we could just take you out right now, then bust in there and do what we came to do."

"You could," I said, by this point fighting to keep the quivering out of my voice. Wouldn't do much for the old tough guy image, not to mention my own confidence in myself, if my voice started cracking. "Though I don't think Marcus would like that. Not his style. Too much noise and hassle for too little. Far as that goes, I'm a little surprised that he's not with you. He didn't impress me as the kind of guy who would farm work out to the minor leagues. As it is, you all have pretty much mucked up this whole thing."

"Mucked up?" Redhead snorted. "Old man, you don't even know what the thing is."

"No, but I'm starting to get a pretty good idea. Don't you think you guys are getting a little carried away, though? How many more bodies do the Hamptons expect to pile up? Especially since you don't have Sheila to blame them on now?"

"Why don't all of us just . . ."

The elevator dinged, and the doors slid open as an elderly man and woman, the man wearing a gray suit and the woman a long, navy blue dress, walked out into the corridor. Almost instantaneously, the blond guy closest to the elevators reached out and snared the old woman around the neck, in the same motion a 9mm coming out from behind his back.

At the same time, the redhead did a 180 and straight-armed the old man back into the elevator just as the doors slid shut.

The third member of the bully boys was also whipping out a weapon, this one leveling up to eventually point directly at me.

Provided I didn't move out of the way, which I proceeded to do.

I didn't know why the guys spooked the way they did, and at the moment didn't care. Crouching down to lose a couple of inches of height, I surged forward and did my own straight-arm move, sending the redhead smack into the now-closed elevator doors. His body crumped against the hard steel, then slid down to the ground, leaving a faint red smear on the metal door as he did so.

Out of the corner of my eye, I saw the woman hostage beginning to have a freak-out. I wheeled back around to confront the guy holding her, at the same time drawing my own weapon to bring it into the fray.

The lady was jittering and shaking all over the place so much so that even the young buck was having a difficult time keeping her under control. I figured he would be distracted for a second or so, allowing me time to continue my turn and face down the remaining member of the trio.

Unfortunately, as I turned and leveled my gun the third one had been course-correcting his own track, and the two of us ended up staring each other down over our weapons.

"Playtime's over, sport," I said. "My friend's calling the cops, and since we're only about eight blocks from the station, straight down Main Street, they'll be here in no time at all."

"We have a hostage," the blond said.

I glanced over at the other pair. The woman had pretty much run out of steam and slumped in her captor's arms. The indicator light over the elevator door began shooting upwards.

"Maybe," I said, "but who's to say who's coming up in that cage. The old man's surely bringing reinforcements, maybe a security guard or two, and while you two could possibly take all of us, my guess is that Marcus, let alone George and Mary, don't want a bloodbath in a local establishment. Seems to me they have enough troubles as it is."

Just then, the redhead, slumped unconscious on the floor all through this, groaned and rolled half over. He wasn't awake yet, though he would be in no time at all.

"What are you suggesting?" the blond staring me down asked. His companion hadn't said a word, merely glanced back and forth between the two of us as we conversed.

The indicator light showed the cage was only two floors below us.

"I'm suggesting," I said, "that you may want to take the stairs at the end of the hall there and get the heck out of here before things get worse. You'll have to explain to Marcus why you ran off, which I guess would be better than explaining a massacre in the middle of downtown."

The redhead groaned again, and his eyes fluttered. Before he could focus though, the blond bearing down on me made the decision.

"Fuck this," he said to his buddy. The other one tossed the old woman, almost catatonic by this point, to the ground. I lowered my weapon, making the move as non-threatening as I could, and together they grabbed their semi-conscious friend under the armpits and prepared to heft him up.

Turned out they'd waited too long though, because just as they'd begun easing down the hall the elevator swooshed open, revealing Josh Nichols and three uniformed cops, all four with drawn weapons.

I flung myself towards the woman, as gingerly as possible covering her in case actual shooting started.

The two thugs, their weapons down and arms full with their buddy, didn't have a chance.

And they knew it.

They dropped the redhead to the floor, managing to thump his head again, as they raised their arms.

Behind me, the door to Karyn's room opened up.

"Is it okay to come out now, boys?" she asked.

CHAPTER FORTY-ONE

"**Y**OU GOT LUCKY," Nichols told me a couple of minutes later.
"I prefer to think of it as brave, determined and resourceful," I said.

"Naw, more like lucky."

We were in Karyn's hotel room while several other cops milled around in the hall doing whatever cops do at an almost-crime scene. The old woman had been taken away, and I assumed her husband was attending to her. The three goons, last I saw, were arrayed along one of the hallway walls, cuffed and waiting to be hauled off.

Nichols and I had scooted to the privacy of Karyn's room to hash things over. It took me all of four minutes to give him the full story.

"Uh huh," he'd commented, "and just why do you suppose they came here after Ms. Roberts?"

This whole time, Karyn had sat on a nearby sofa, her laptop propped open on the coffee table in front of her. She'd watched us intently, keeping quiet the whole time.

"Well," I'd scratched my head as I'd mused over how much to tell Nichols, "I think it's like this." Then I'd basically laid out my "Sheila Hampton framed by everyone in the world" theory.

"Uh huh," Nichols had fallen into the habit of repeating himself. "What are you really saying?"

"Geez, Josh, I thought you were a detective."

"I am, Blondie. And this detective can see one huge hole in your theory."

"Oh, yeah." I'd decided to challenge him with high-brow language. "What's that?"

"If the Hamptons were behind killing their brother, and framing Sheila, then killing Harris 'cause he was going to spill the beans, once we put Sheila in jail aren't they blowing the whole idea by trying to knock off everyone else in town?"

I mulled that one over for a minute.

"Okay. Maybe I haven't thought it all the way through."

"I'll say." Nichols didn't do a very good job of concealing the sarcasm in his tone.

"Maybe they're panicking," Karyn spoke up from the couch. We turned in her direction. "Maybe they're losing control and flailing around."

"You ever meet Mary Hampton?" Nichols asked her.

Karyn shook her head. "Never had the pleasure. I tried to interview both of them, back when during the original case, but they stonewalled me."

"Let's just say that the last thing Mary Hampton would do is lose control. There's stories of her firing presidents of their companies just because they forgot to call her ma'am."

"How does George act?" I asked.

"You met them, right?" Nichols asked.

"I did, and Mary did the majority of the talking."

"How'd she treat you?"

"Like I was something she'd forgotten to scrape off her shoe."

"There you go. And from what I hear I'll bet George was mister nice and polite the whole time."

"She did seem to kind of dominate things a bit," I said. "I'd almost wonder if she, or her brother, weren't flat-out sociopaths."

"Meaning they enjoy screwing with people's lives?" Karyn asked.

"Well, if you think about it, they've got the means and resources to do so. Not to mention the money and connections to keep their activity under the radar as far as the public's concerned."

"How exactly do you propose to handle them?" Nichol asked.

"By getting enough to bust them good," I said.

"Yeah, big guy. But how?"

"Uh, about that," I said, grinning ruefully, "we're trying to work that out."

CHAPTER FORTY-TWO

A S IT TURNED OUT, THAT NEXT STEP was going to be easier than I thought.

There'd been enough of a ruckus raised at the hotel that Nichols called in and received permission from Lt. Santiago to get a couple of uniforms to keep an eye on Karyn. To be even more cautious, we placed her in a new room on a different floor.

While I was all for spiriting her off to a different hotel, Karyn nixed that idea, and the lieutenant didn't think it was all that necessary.

Feeling a bit more relieved, though only a bit, I headed out to take care of a few things.

My next step was back to The Blaster to check in on things. With early evening coming on, the gym was almost filled up with an assortment of clients. Most periods of the day were marked by certain categories of clients: early morning by late shifters coming off work; real early morning by retirees with too much time on their hands; the noon hour by business professionals; and mid-afternoon by harried, upper-class mothers who didn't need to bother with a job yet could afford nannies.

Early evening, however, always presented a mixed bag, all shapes, sorts and sizes, getting in their personally required amount of exertion for the week. Lisa and Keri were both there, both scurrying all around the place, and as soon as I walked in Lisa headed my direction, shooting me a dirty look from all the way across the gym.

"We could use some help," she said as she came within earshot, "but I guess that's out of the question, huh?"

"Excuse me?"

"Somebody waiting on you. Said you were expecting him."

I rolled through my memory, for the life of me unable to remember any sort of appointment I had.

"The office?" I asked after drawing a blank.

Lisa nodded, then hustled off to help someone waving at her from one of the juice dispensers she'd recently installed.

I remembered my youth, the hard-scrabble gyms I worked out in, where if someone had asked for a can of juice they would have been laughed out of the room, then blackballed from ever returning again.

One of the reasons I've resisted, against better judgement, from stepping back and letting Lisa run the whole show is the fear of just how modernized the place would get.

I went off to the back part, towards my office, wondering just who was waiting for me. I briefly debated heading back out to the car and grabbing my gun then decided I'd feel silly if the only thing lurking in wait was a saleslady for a new type of protein drink.

As soon as I opened the door, I'd wished I'd taken the cautious route.

It sure looked like a thug sitting in one of my client chairs.

CHAPTER FORTY-THREE

I CLOSED THE DOOR AND WITHOUT A WORD walked over and sat behind my desk. The guy waiting on me looked about six foot or so, but it was kind of hard to tell with him sitting down. He had an almost phony-looking tan. His dark hair was coated in some sort of jell, and his arms and shoulders nearly tore the seams of his black silk tee-shirt.

He didn't introduce himself, merely stared at me. I got right down to business.

"Do something for you?" I said as I rested my right hand on the handle of my middle desk drawer.

"You the guy who used to wrestle?"

His voice was deep, full, almost like an opera singer's.

"Sam Quinton," I said. "What do you want?"

The muscular man stood up, and my hand gripped the drawer handle a little tighter.

Then, quick as you could think, he whipped his hand to his back pocket and pulled out a plain, white envelope.

Taking one step forward, he dropped the envelope on my desk.

"Guy told me to give this to you."

I sat motionless. Though the envelope was sealed, it looked empty.

"What guy?" I asked.

The guy shook his head. "Not for you to know. He said you'd want it and that after I give it to you I'm to take off. No questions answered."

"Well," I said, "I am a little short on empty envelopes that have already been sealed. Thanks, I guess."

The thuggish-looking man shook his head. "Some people aren't nearly as funny as they think they are."

He turned and left the office, and only after the door had closed all the way did I pull my hand away from the center drawer.

I had no need for the gun now.

Picking the envelope up, I felt a slight weight inside of it.

Too light to be a bomb. Even too light to be a letter from George and Mary telling me to back off.

Mentally shrugging, I ripped open the flap.

A small, tan colored business card dropped out.

Though the name, number and e-mail of the person who owned the card had been blacked out, the place of business was still legible.

The Second Bank of Jefferson County.

I turned the card over and saw that someone had written a message in block letters with a red pen.

"Looking for something?" the message said.

"Gotcha," I exclaimed to my empty office.

CHAPTER FORTY-FOUR

I PICKED KARYN UP AT HER HOTEL Tuesday morning, and we climbed into the Cherokee for the ride down to the state capital.

The night before, after my mysterious visitor left, I'd managed to get ahold of Bernie and explained what I needed and why I needed it, then spent the rest of the night puttering around The Blaster and trying to make myself look useful.

The next morning, Bernie called first thing and announced he'd managed to get a court order for Robert Harris's safe deposit box, and agreed to meet me and Karyn down at the bank around eleven. He had some evidentiary hearings in Sheila's case, but they weren't until the afternoon, and if everything went exactly right well before then we'd have enough new evidence to blow everything else to hell

Maybe.

Of course, the three of us could have driven down to the Jeff City bank together. I hadn't suggested that to Bernie, seeing as I wanted some more time to get to know Karyn. Turned out, she spent most of the time on her I-Pad doing work.

Possibly I should have taken the time to shave that morning.

At one point, about halfway to the capital, she looked up from her work.

"I didn't sleep very well last night," she said.

"Scared?" I asked.

Karyn looked straight ahead and said, "yes."

"Understandable," I added a few seconds later. "It would have scared anyone, provided they had common sense."

"In all the time I covered local news, all the extra legal work I've done, I've never been in a situation like that."

I didn't know what to say.

"Are you used to that kind of thing?" she said a moment later.

"Not all that much really. Most of my work is on the low end of things. Company fraud, skip tracing, stuff like that."

"There was the deal with the mobsters last spring?"

"Yeah," I said as I rolled my shoulders a bit. They'd become tense. "That was a little hairy, but you know . . ."

"You just trying to be all manly and macho to get me to like you?" she asked. Out of the corner of my eye, I could see a bit of a grin on her face.

"Never hurts to try," I said.

Before she could respond, I made a turn into Jeff City's downtown area and we arrived at our destination.

A few minutes later, we walked into the Second Bank of Jefferson County at eleven straight up and saw Bernie sitting on a maroon easy chair in the lobby. With the noon hour closing in, several customers milled around the place, either standing in line at the tellers' windows or sitting talking to the various customer service people at their desks.

I didn't see anyone who looked under fifty and wondered how many people thirty-five or younger had never even been inside a bank.

Bernie stood up and came our way, a legal-looking blue binder in his hand.

"That it?" I asked.

"Yep. Court order allowing us to open and inspect the contents of Mr. Harris's box, provided he has one here."

"If he doesn't, I don't know where else it would be. Are you sure that order's entirely legal, Bern?"

"As legal as it needs to be," he said, which didn't ease my mind a whole lot. "What I'm wondering is just who's our benefactor."

"Meaning?"

"Meaning just who paid your visitor yesterday to give you that card."

"Waitaminit," Karyn said at my side. "You don't know who told you what bank to come to?"

"Actually," I said, "I've got a few theories, but at the moment what does it matter?"

"What does it matter?" She shook her head, her eyes downcast. "How do we know this isn't some big misdirection here?"

"Even if it is, so what? What have we lost? A couple of hours? And what if it isn't?"

Neither one of them had anything to say to that. Instead, Bernie raised his hand to wave at someone behind us. A moment later, an attractive brunette woman in her late thirties, wearing a light gray skirt and black blouse, came up to us.

"This is Miss London. She's going to escort us into the deposit box room."

I smiled at Miss London. If I hadn't been wearing a lightweight blazer, I would have made a muscle.

She smiled at me.

Maybe I should stick with not shaving.

Karyn Roberts rolled her eyes.

With Miss London in the lead, the four of us trotted up a flight of stairs and towards the back of the building. A few seconds later we were standing at a table with a long, rectangular metal box in front of us. Miss London excused herself and left the room.

"Okay, then," I said as I pulled the key out of my pocket and opened the box.

That simple.

Nothing to it.

Taking a deep breath, I reached in and pulled out a bundle of five sealed manila envelopes. Spreading them out on the table, we could see that each one had a name written in black ink.

Mike Palmer, Lois Jackson, Leslie Brown, Robert Harris.

All the main participants in the Sheila Hampton trial twenty-five years before.

Plus one more.

I glanced at Bernie out of the corner of my eye. A tic had developed in his left cheek. Other than that he showed nothing.

"It may not be what it looks like," I said to him.

Bernie didn't look at me. Instead he kept staring at the name on that final envelope, focused so intensely he should have been able to melt the metal the table was made of.

As soon as I'd pulled the envelope out and placed it on the table, I'd known that Bernie was in for a bad day.

The name on the final envelope was Howard Landon.

CHAPTER FORTY-FIVE

Each envelope contained an affidavit, written by Robert Harris and notarized by a notary public. Most of them were several pages long. Each of us took one and began reading. I chose the one concerning Mike Palmer; Bernie picked the one with Judge Jackson's name; and Karyn began reading about Detective Lewis Thomas. The bank's deposit room had some comfortable chairs scattered around, and before long each of us had sat down and focused on our reading.

It didn't take long before Bernie stood up, went over to the table and switched the Jackson affidavit for the envelope with Harris's name at the top. I wondered if he were deliberately avoiding the packet with Landon's name, but decided not to ask.

After about twenty minutes, almost by consent, the three of us set aside our reading material and looked at each other.

"It seems," Bernie began, "that Lois Jackson's son was involved in an incident with a girl at his school."

"College?" I asked.

"No. High school. A private one."

"Yeah?"

"Yeah," Bernie said. "And the young girl was hospitalized from injuries sustained."

"He assaulted her?" I asked, remembering his attack on Karyn a few nights back.

Bernie continued reading for a minute before looking up again.

"Hard to say. According to the affidavit the girl was only fourteen, and it happened when the Jackson boy was fifteen. Who can tell if it was consensual or not?"

"What's the age of consent in Missouri?" Karyn asked.

"Seventeen."

"Back then?" I asked.

Bernie nodded.

"Was the kid ever charged with anything?" Karyn asked.

Bernie shook his head. "According to this, it was hushed up pretty well. The hospital stay was labeled as treatment for a flu."

"Uh huh," Karyn muttered, possibly herself remembering her encounter with Carson Jackson.

"And Jackson's kid went scot free," I said.

Bernie turned to Karyn. "All this about a year before Sheila was tried for killing Derek. What about yours?"

"It talks about a police incident back in the nineties, when two cops answered a robbery call at a convenience store. One of the officers who responded was Leslie Brown."

"He hadn't made detective yet?"

"He was just about to. There was a shootout as the robbers were leaving the store, and a pregnant woman was caught in the cross-fire. She and the baby died."

"So?" I almost didn't want to hear the rest.

"According to the official report, one of the robbers fired the bullet that killed the woman and her baby." Karyn paused to tap the folder in front of her. "According to this affidavit, it was the senior officer on scene, Thomas's partner, Andrew Garibaldi."

Bernie shook his head.

I glanced his way. "Am I missing something?"

"You would have been gone from town by then, Blondie. Either that or you were a teenager. You could be forgiven for not recognizing the name." He looked over at Karyn. "Is it who I think it was?"

Karyn nodded while I still felt out of the loop.

"I'm guessing," Bernie said, "that Andrew Garibaldi was the son of Thomas Garibaldi. At the time, Providence's police chief."

Now it was my turn to groan. "And if my math is right, this was shortly before Brown was promoted up to detective."

"And about a year before he was handed the biggest case of his life," Karyn pointed out.

"The Hampton case," I said, just to keep there from being too much quiet.

"What about yours?" Karyn asked, pointing to the affidavit on Palmer.

I shook my head. "The supercop Mike Palmer wasn't all he was cracked up to be."

"I'm shocked."

"Yeah," I said, noticing Bernie peering at me. "He was on the take. According to this, to just about anyone in town who had the money, primarily drug dealers."

"But he was in uniform his entire career," Karyn said. "What could he have done for . . ."

"Notifications," Bernie interrupted.

"Right. He had a habit of tipping the gangs off whenever a bust was coming down," I said. "Since he was one of the senior guys in the patrol division, the detectives usually went through him to coordinate uniforms to help them in their busts."

"Jesus Christ," Karyn whispered.

For once, I didn't feel like cracking a joke or brushing anything off. I gestured towards the envelopes and papers spread out before us. "You know what Harris had here, right?"

"Dirty little secrets, skeletons in the closet, of all the principals involved in Sheila's case," Bernie said.

"And if Harris had this information," Karyn said.

"It's a good bet that George and Mary Hampton had it as well. Geez, these people are devious as hell."

"Who was the original corruptor?" Karyn asked. "Did Harris get it from them or did they get it from Harris?"

Before I could respond, Bernie's eyes drifted again to the one unopened envelope on the table.

"Bern," I said, "we have enough here. No need to look any . . ."

"I need to know, Sam. I need to get it cleared up once and for . . ."

My phone beeped, and Bernie stopped talking. I pulled it out of my pocket, looked at the message and, despite the seriousness of what we had discovered, couldn't help but grin.

"What is it?" Karyn asked.

"The ruckus I've been raising the last few days," I said. "I think it's starting to pay off."

CHAPTER FORTY-SIX

I ARRIVED AT THE STATION A LITTLE after two.

Going up to the detective's bureau gave me some qualms. I used to hang out there quite frequently. Not enough to make a nuisance of myself, as far as I knew, but enough that I knew most of the men and women up there, even those who didn't work out at The Blaster, on a first name basis. But my second time up there after the whole Kronberg/ O'Brien fiasco made it clear that I wasn't wanted around, and that my continued presence would only end up hurting Josh Nichols.

As far as I knew, Nichols himself had suffered no recriminations from his fellow cops. Most good cops hate the bad ones even more than regular citizens do. Nichols, who'd been popular on the force before the whole mess, was well liked by his colleagues.

I was a slightly different matter, though. I was a civilian, and as such was more suspect. True, none of them stopped coming by the gym and sharing a friendly word with me, but in the confines of their own house, the reception was a little more frosty. Enough that I'd stopped coming around unless I absolutely had to.

What the hell. No big loss. My buddy was okay with his fellows and grouching over the whole deal wouldn't help matters any. On this day, however, I had a solid reason for showing up in the bureau, even if I wasn't exactly thrilled to be doing so.

When I entered the main floor, a young, bright-faced kid named Kenny Landrun, whose desk was closest to the door, grinned at me and crooked his finger towards the back corner, where the only completely enclosed office on the whole floor sat.

Landrun didn't have to direct me. I knew where I was going. I gave the guy a grin and a wave and headed to the lieutenant's office.

The blinds were drawn. I knocked, and after a minute Nichols opened the door.

"Come on in, Sam," he said as he stood aside for me.

Crammed into the ten by twenty-foot space were Josh, Lt. Santiago, George and Mary Hampton, their bully boy Marcus, and three men in dark gray suits with blue ties.

The three guys in suits each held a briefcase, from which I deduced they were lawyers. And since they dressed too well to work for the city, and they didn't work for me, I further assumed they belonged to the Hamptons.

Uh huh.

"Afternoon, Josh. Lieutenant." I looked in Santiago's direction while ignoring the Hampton party. "What can I do for you?"

"Take a seat, Mr. Quinton," Santiago said. Today he was wearing a tan poplin suit with a navy tie. His hair looked perfectly groomed, and his nails shown like he'd just come from a manicurist.

What the hell was it with this guy?

I looked around at everyone else. With everyone standing around, the one chair in the room, directly in front of Santiago's desk, looked a little too much like a bullseye to me.

"Thanks, lieutenant. I think I'll stand."

The boss cop looked as if it couldn't make a damn to him. "Reason I asked you to come down, Quinton, is that Mr. Hampton and his sister here are talking about filing charges against you, and I thought it may help to talk things over first."

"Which I'm against," George Hampton said, his bushy white eyebrows wriggling across his face. "I think I want to just proffer charges against this man."

In my jeans and tee-shirt, I was the most underdressed person in the meeting. I tried not to let that bother me.

"Proffer charges?" Santiago's voice went up about half a pitch. "Who the hell says proffer charges?"

Hampton took a step back, his face looking like he'd been slapped.

Probably not used to the little people speaking to him like that.

I tried to take in both Santiago and Nichols at the same time. Both of them were wearing poker faces.

"Excuse me, lieutenant?" George Hampton said as politely as he could, his sister visibly seething at his side.

"Not a problem, Mr. Hampton. I just don't see the reason for any fancy talk in this matter. Even if you did bring the three suits with you."

George's face turned a faint shade of red while Mary grimaced.

"I don't believe I understand, Santiago," Mary said. "Just what it is you . . ."

"That's okay, ma'am, because there's a lot about this I don't understand either. And as long as we're striving for an understanding and all that, it's Lieutenant Santiago to you."

The lieutenant's voice had dropped about ten degrees, causing the temperature in the office to decline as well.

After several heartbeats of silence, Santiago spoke up again. "Now then, from what I understand, see how I'm trying, you're accusing Mr. Quinton of harassing you and your brother, correct?"

"That's right."

"And just what form did this harassment take?"

"He was surveilling our property." Mary pointed her finger at me.

The lieutenant looked my way. "That true, Quinton?"

"Sure," I said. George and Mary began beaming, feeling the situation coming under their control. "If you call driving and parking on a public street surveilling, I guess I was."

Santiago turned his gaze back on the Hamptons. Other than his initial greeting, Nichols hadn't said a word since I entered.

"How about that, folks?" the lieutenant asked.

George's smile slipped a bit. "He's also been publicly impugning our reputations." His voice cracked on the last syllable.

The three blind mice with their briefcases hadn't said a word.

Santiago cocked an eye my way.

I said. "I'm just an ex-jock, lieutenant. I don't even know what impugning means. All I've been doing the last few days is lawfully investigating a possible crime, as my license from the state permits me to do."

"That license could become awfully slippery, mister," one of the lawyers spoke up.

I turned full face to George and Mary for the first time since I'd entered the office. "That's pretty good, Mary. I didn't even see your lips move. But could you make your boy there sound less like he'd walked out of a *Goodfellows* script?"

Her face turned bright red, and she turned full to Santiago. The lawyer who had spoken looked confused.

"What are you going to do about this, lieutenant?" Mary asked.

Santiago glanced my way, then at his sergeant. "You have any input, Nichols?"

"No, sir."

"Okay, then. Mr. Hampton, Miss Hampton, here's what I'm going to do. I'm going to warn Mr. Quinton, in the strongest possible terms, to make sure he doesn't in any way break the law. I'm going to emphasize to him that his investigator's license is revocable if he does in any way break the law. Then I'm going to go about the business that's piled up on my desk; Sergeant Nichols here is going to go about his business; and the two of you, along with your three mannequins there, are going to get the hell out of my office. Is that clear?"

The crimson in Mary's face had gone completely off the lividity scale while George just looked kind of benumbed by the whole thing.

"You're making a mistake here, lieutenant," Mary said, her voice regulated down a bit from the earlier hiss. "Someone higher up may not look kindly on your cavalier attitude towards a couple of citizens being harassed by this . . . this . . ."

"Meathead?" I added helpfully.

"I may be making a mistake," Santiago put in before either of the Hamptons could reply to me. He stood up behind his desk. "But I doubt it. The truth is, while you and your brother, and your lackeys, may think you're all something special, back in Chicago I know people who could eat you folks for lunch without even burping. And I didn't take any shit from them either."

It occurred to me that, his flippant words notwithstanding, something had derailed Santiago from the fast track in Chicago and landed him in little old Providence. There was a particular bitterness in his voice.

Since the head cop seemed to be taking my side, I decided not to speak up.

George and Mary had run out of words as well. Or at least, Mary had. George had barely spoken since I'd entered the lieutenant's office and now cast a look at the three briefcase holders, flicked his eyes toward the door and headed out. As the five of them ushered out of the squad room, mustering what dignity they could, I glanced at Josh, flicking my eyes momentarily in Santiago's direction.

Josh gave me a look.

"Quinton," the lieutenant said as the door swung shut behind the chastened group, "I'm guessing you can tell I don't care much for rich people and their lawyers."

"I kind of noticed that, lieutenant."

"'Course you did. But understand this at the same time. I don't care for private licenses who raise problems in my jurisdiction. If you've got a job to do, do it. I can't stop you there. On the other hand, I don't want those two knocking on my door every other day. Understood?"

I turned full on to Santiago and gave him my best rendition of the "aw shucks" grin. "Understood, lieutenant. I'll try my best to keep a low profile."

"You do that. And while you're trying your best, get the hell out of my office and my station house."

I really needed to work on the "aw shucks."

CHAPTER FORTY-SEVEN

A FTER LEAVING THE STATION, I placed a quick call to Bernie's cell. Not getting an answer, I turned around and called Karyn. She picked up on the first ring. "Hello?"

"It's me. Where are you?"

"Just got back to my hotel. I offered to go back with Mr. Lyman to his office, but he turned me down."

"Go back with him why?"

"He was very upset after reading that final affidavit. I'm guessing he looked up to Howard Landon quite a bit."

"He did," I said. "Saw him as the last of the old-time crusaders. A regular Atticus Finch." I paused to see if she'd be impressed by my literary knowledge. When she said nothing, I continued on. "How bad was it?"

"Why don't you come pick me up and we can grab lunch?"

"I've a better idea," I said. "I'm standing about a block away from the police station, once again staring at my all-time favorite BBQ place. Now's the chance for me to prove to you that Providence is in the running with KC."

She laughed, and it felt good to hear. "Okay, tiger. Tell me where and I'll see you in a few minutes."

"JESUS," I SAID ABOUT TWENTY MINUTES LATER. "For real?"

Karyn nodded and dug further into her brisket sandwich. I toyed with my beans and coleslaw, but had lost my appetite.

"How did Landon get into that fix?" I asked.

Karyn finished chewing and took a drink of her Dr Pepper. "It was a client, or possibly former client. Name was Linda Cummings. No doubt a professional name. According to the affidavit, Landon had represented her a handful of times on soliciting busts."

"Was he being paid in trade?" I asked.

Karyn cocked her head. "Nothing about that in the document. There was mention that he didn't charge her for his legal work, so who knows?"

I tried visualizing an aging defense lawyer with a hooker. Knowing how highly Bernie thought of Landon made the idea hard to stomach.

"What was the actual hold?" I asked. "What exactly did they have on him?"

Karyn pushed her plate away, though her food was only half eaten. "You're right," she said. "It is really good here."

"Karyn."

She brushed a stray lock of her out of her eyes. "The Cummings woman claimed that Landon beat her up once after he got her off of some charges. Said she asked him to wait a couple of days to take his 'payment,' and he became incensed and assaulted her so badly he put her in the hospital."

"Any actual evidence of that?" I asked.

Karyn answered. "Supposedly there's copies of hospital records, though in the affidavit she doesn't say who has them."

I mulled that over for a while, trying to wrap my head around just how sick the whole thing was.

"Christ," Karyn said. "Sheila never had a chance. At Amendment V we went over the trial transcripts, but we just thought Landon did a piss poor job. If he threw the trial for the state, he did it in a pretty damned masterful way. If he was that good of an attorney, he should have been able to get her off, at least on appeal, even with all the others compromised. He never even bothered to file a single appeal. On a capital case, of all things."

"A heel turn," I muttered.

"Come again?"

I stopped toying with my food and looked up at her. "It's a term from my wrestling days. In pro wrestling, there's good guys and bad guys, what we call faces and heels. And every now and then, to move the story along, a good guy, a face, turns bad."

"He turns into a heel."

"Right. Which is why we call it a heel turn."

"This isn't playacting, goddammit," Karyn said. "This is real life. And just because those two screwed Sheila over once, that's no reason to let them do it again."

As I mulled over Karyn's words, it occurred to me that I'd finally come to a realization in this case. For the first time, I was wholly convinced that Sheila Hampton was innocent of the original charge.

"I don't think there's much chance of that," I said. "They've basically screwed the pooch on this whole thing. Either George or Mary, or maybe both of them, has gone completely around the bend."

"Then what do we do about it?" Karyn asked.

"Let's go," I said, getting up and picking up my tray.

"Where?"

"To make sure those two get what they have coming to them."

CHAPTER FORTY-EIGHT

I CALLED BERNIE AND CHATTED WITH HIM A BIT. He sounded subdued, and I guessed he hadn't yet worked through the tarnishing of his mentor's image. I pointed out that the allegations against Landon could have been wholly made up. It didn't seem to satisfy him.

"You talked to Sheila lately?" I asked.

"I have. And she's just as pleasant as always. Wanted to know why she was still sitting in jail."

"You explain the whole no-bail-on-a-capital-case thing?" I asked.

"Only for about the eightieth time, at least it seems like that many. I'm telling you, Sam, if she was this unpleasant back when, I'm surprised they even had to threaten Howard to throw the case."

I let the bitterness pass, assuming that Bernie would take some time to work through his issues.

"If you want to, tell her to hang in there. I've a feeling this whole thing may wrap pretty soon."

We left Bernie to do what he could on the legal end and headed back down to Jeff City. Getting on in the afternoon, traffic had picked up a bit. It took Karyn and me about forty-five minutes to get to our destination. As we pulled up outside the house, she shook her head.

"You planning on waiting?" she asked. "It's the middle of a weekday. She's bound to be at work now."

I took a moment to scope out the lay of the land. Didn't see any obvious villains lurking around, which I took for a good sign.

But I'm a PI, not an urban commando. There could have been scads of trained people spying on me right that moment and I wouldn't have known it.

"I'm betting she's not," I said. "No matter how you look at it, this thing's starting to fall apart. I'm guessing she won't want to be anywhere too public for a while."

"You're just guessing."

I grinned, not the full-wattage smile I gave women when I was younger and studlier but close enough. "Kind of. Before we left, when you stepped into the ladies room, I called the courthouse and they said she was out for the day."

"Called in sick?"

"Wouldn't tell me a reason, and it would have been worthless to press it. It was enough to know that she's not there."

"Doesn't mean she's home. She could have taken off for somewhere."

"True. I'd say there's at least a fifty/fifty chance she's holed up."

Karyn shook her head. I wondered if she was deliberately disagreeing just for the hell of it. "If she's afraid for her life, or whatever, wouldn't she have gone to the state cops, or even the governor, and gotten some sort of protection detail? How are you going to get to her?"

Okay, maybe the lady a had a point. I skulled that one over for a few minutes as the bright September afternoon crept by.

"Not necessarily," I pointed out. "If she was an ordinary judge facing some sort of threat, sure. That'd be the smart thing to do. But if we're right, then that kind of attention is the last thing she'd want."

Karyn said, "True, though there's one other thing to consider."

"Which is?"

"Have you forgotten about Carson?"

"No," I said, "I haven't. If he comes up, we'll deal with him. After the other night, I doubt he'll give me much trouble. I'm going to try to get in there and talk to the judge. You coming or you want to wait here for me?"

"Oh, sure. Wait out here for some goons to come along and take me out? Don't think so. Just tell me one thing, mister. How exactly are you going to get her to talk to us?"

I cracked open my door. "You know I was a professional wrestler for several years, right?"

"So I hear. And?"

"Half of being a wrestler is getting the crowd to either love or hate you, depending on how the script's written."

She frowned. "I don't quite follow."

I grinned. "It's all psychology, Karyn. Being able to sell the audience on your character. Trust me, I'm one hell of a salesman."

"Uh huh."

I DIDN'T EXPECT THE JUDGE TO ANSWER A KNOCK on her door, and in fact she didn't. Karyn walked up, gave a couple of quick raps, then stood waiting for some response.

While she waited, Judge Jackson eased open the back door to her house, stepped through the sliding doors and onto her patio and, looking back and focusing her attention the way she'd come out, damned near plowed into me.

The lady shrieked then managed to stifle it almost immediately when I grabbed her by the arms. She looked up at me, her face drawn and pale under the gray hair.

"You—you—" she stammered a couple more times before she got it together and quieted down.

The latch on the back of her redwood gate opened up, and Karyn stepped through.

"You have her?" she called out.

Before I could answer, another commotion started up in the house.

"Mom? What the hell is . . ."

Carson Jackson stepped out, took one look at the scene in front of him, and did the natural and manly thing.

He jumped out onto the patio and made a beeline straight for me, the guy with hands on his mom.

I eased the judge back and to the side and met Carson's rush

head on. It didn't take much. In his hurry, I'm not sure if he recognized me or not. Either way didn't seem to matter. He thrust
out his right hand, trying for a very clumsy roundhouse. I ducked
under, whirled aside and tapped him one in the right kidney.

It honestly wasn't that hard of a punch, but the kid froze, glanced
at his mother for a minute, then dropped to the ground.

He lay there gasping and clawing a little at the concrete.

I waited. Judge Jackson stood there, her eyes on her son, but
made no move to go to him. It was a curious reaction, and I
glanced at Karyn, who found it just as odd. After a moment, the
judge shook her head and sat down in a nearby lawn chair.

Well, okay.

"Judge," I said, "don't you think there's been just about enough
of this?"

She clasped her hands in front of her and lowered her head,
her shoulder blades standing out in tension against the thin yellow
blouse she wore. I looked again at Karyn, who shook her head at
me, then down at big, bad Carson, lying there kind of gasping on
the ground.

"Judge?" I prodded again.

She looked up, her eyes faintly glistening.

"I'm tired," she said. "I am goddamned tired of all of it. What do
you want from me? What are you doing here?"

"Sheila Hampton," I said. Before she could answer, her son
began moaning.

"Mom," he said, raising himself half up. I gave the kid a look,
and he slumped back down.

The judge barely glanced at him.

"A life for a life," she murmured. "I am so sick of this."

I continued waiting, a bit disappointed that she may have
already cracked and I wouldn't get the chance to try the smart play
I'd worked out.

A long, nearly explosive sigh, and the lady stood up.

"Let's go inside," she said, "I guess there's some things you
should know."

CHAPTER FORTY-NINE

For a minute there, I thought she was going to leave her son to fend for himself. Then she went over, helped him up, spoke to him quietly for a few minutes, then motioned us into her house. Carson came in behind us, me keeping one eye on him, but as soon as we got inside he headed off upstairs, while the three of us went into the living room and sat down. The judge took an easy chair that faced a couch where Karyn and I sat.

For a minute, the three of us just sat there, almost like an awkward social encounter. Then the judge leaned back and closed her eyes.

"I have a lot to make up for," she said without opening her eyes.

"Such as?" I asked.

She leaned farther back. "Such as what happened to that poor girl."

"You mean Sheila Hampton?"

She nodded. I couldn't quite tell, but it looked as if a few faint tears were seeping past her closed lids. She squeezed her eyes even tighter, then sat up and looked at us.

"Understand one thing. I would never have done what I did if I hadn't honestly believed she was guilty. I'm not saying that as rationalization. Judges aren't supposed to worry about guilt or innocence, just whether or not the process is followed. We're kind of like umpires that way."

"Judge," Karyn broke in, "before you say anything more, I should tell you something. My name's Karyn Roberts and I work with . . ."

"I know who you are, Ms. Roberts. Believe me, over the last few months I've made it a point to become well acquainted with your group. Thanks for trying to warn me. It's actually more than I deserve."

Karyn leaned back, looking a bit chastened. After months, maybe years, of chasing the big bad wolf, she'd caught her at last, and realized the wolf was just another screwed up person, like most of us.

"You were saying, judge?" I prodded.

Judge Jackson took a deep breath. "I ran Mrs. Hampton's trial by the letter of the law, the strictest letter. I didn't in any way violate the exact wording of any statute."

"But?"

Another deep breath, and the eyes started to glisten again. "There were several times where I could have reasonably seen a particular motion or objection the defense's way, times where deep down I wanted to, and each of those times I went with the prosecution."

"Because you felt she was guilty and wanted to put your thumb on the scale?" I asked, not quite able to keep a cutting tone out of my voice.

The lady shook her head and, for an instant, glanced upwards, in the direction her son had headed when we entered the house.

"No," she said. "For him. For Carson."

I realized I was holding my breath and, glancing over at Karyn, saw she was doing the same. I forced myself to breathe and keep the conversation going.

"I don't follow," I said. I did, of course, but wanted to hear it from her

The eyes glistened even more, and she clasped her hands, tightly enough that the tendons stood out.

"When Carson was a teenager there was an—incident—at his school. His father and I had split up a few years before, and he was living with Rick at the time, in St. Louis. Rick called me one Sunday afternoon. Carson had become infatuated with a girl and . . ."

Even all these years later, she couldn't come out and say it. And in a way it wasn't necessary for us to get the point.

Judge Jackson took a deep breath, swiped at her eyes and continued. "Rick was, is, heavily involved in finance. And he knew a lot of people around the county. Important people. We managed to—to—"

"Get it squelched," Karyn almost hissed.

The judge turned to focus on her. "Please understand. It wasn't Carson's fault at all. Just one of those things that happens when young people get together. And there was nothing that anyone. . ."

"Judge," I said. "We've seen the records of what happened."

"And you got it squelched," Karyn repeated.

The judge agreed. "Fine, dammit. We had everything buried. At the time, it felt like the right call. The damage had already been done. We were going to watch him like a hawk afterwards. What was the point in ruining his life?"

Karyn made a noise beside me and turned away.

"Except somehow the Hamptons found out," I said.

The judge nodded again, her eyes turning red. "I don't know how exactly, though I'd always heard rumors about their influence."

"And they used the knowledge to influence you during the trial." I didn't say it as a question.

"Yes," the judge said. "Honestly, though, if you look over the transcripts, you'll see that I didn't make a single call that couldn't be legally justified. I just—hedged a few times."

"Hedged," Karyn said, her tone sarcastic.

"Was it George or Mary?" I asked.

"Huh?"

"Which of them did you deal with? Or was it both?"

"It was Mary. Have you met them?"

I nodded at the same time Karyn shook her head.

"Then you know the dynamic. Between the two, Mary is much more the alpha, probably because their father was an old-fashioned chauvinist and she feels she has to prove something."

"And she loves proving things," I said.

"It was almost like she enjoyed it. She showed up one day when I was having lunch downtown. Her sister-in-law's case had been assigned to me, but we hadn't even started motions yet. She sat down across from me, without permission, and began laying it out."

"Throw the trial or your dirt comes out, right?" I asked.

"More or less. Not in those exact words, but I got the idea."

"Did you report it to anyone?" I asked.

She shook her head. "I thought of doing so. To be honest I was afraid. If she had the power to unearth something hidden that deeply from the other side of the state, what else could she come up with? Who else could she control?"

As it turned out, quite a few people.

"And now we have the answers to that," I said standing up.

Karyn stood with me as the judge looked at us, confusion warring with concern on her face.

"Meaning what?" she asked.

"Come on, judge," Karyn said. "You were there. Did you honestly not notice that everyone else was in the same boat you were?"

Superior Court Judge Lois Jackson lowered her head into her hands.

And I wondered just how many other lives over the years the Hamptons had wrecked.

It felt almost like a family hobby.

CHAPTER FIFTY

I HAD ALL THE PIECES IN PLACE NOW, I just didn't quite know what to do with them. The affidavits, now in Bernie's possession, were fairly strong evidence, but I wasn't lawyer enough to know whether, in and of themselves, they'd hold up in court. At the moment, Jackson seemed willing to testify as a witness; however, a good lawyer, and George and Mary Hampton could no doubt hire the best, would quickly point out that she was coming forward in order to expiate some of her own sins, and we'd be right back to square one.

And even if we laid out all the shenanigans from the first trial, that didn't in and of itself exonerate Sheila from the Harris killing.

It kept coming back to the same thing. If I was going to get this resolved and get Sheila out of jail, not to mention cleared of her first conviction, it had to be the straightforward approach.

And I wasn't looking forward to that.

Karyn and I stayed at the judge's house a bit longer, long enough for the judge to make a call, talk briefly with someone on the other end, then hang up.

"Who'd you call?" I asked.

"A friend of mine with the state police," she said.

"Sgt. Prescott?"

"No, I don't know any Prescott. Besides, the person I called is a bit—higher up than a sergeant."

My earlier visit from the state cop became a bit clearer. I had the impression that Prescott's talk with me hadn't shown up in any official reports. More in the way of a favor for a friend of a friend, and it depended on what the judge had told her contact in her most recent call. I guessed didn't have to worry any more about the intrepid defender of law and order knocking down my door.

Then again, wouldn't hurt to be sure.

"They sending someone over?" I asked.

Judge Jackson said. "A small unit, for protection. I have the right to request it. As soon as I hear from you, or the Providence police, that it's all over I can send them on their way."

I said, "Hopefully won't be too long." We stayed quiet until about ten minutes later when a marked state car pulled up in the drive.

Karyn and I waited long enough for the cops to come in the house, everyone to introduce themselves, and make sure the judge was in good hands, then we headed out to my Cherokee and proceeded on our way.

Karyn settled back in her seat.

"What now?" she asked.

"I need a wedge. Something I can pull at that will bring the whole thing down. If I can do that, Sheila may come out in the wash entirely. For both now and back then."

"And how will you find this wedge?" Karyn asked.

"I figure out a way to get at the Hamptons, which isn't going to be easy."

"I thought they were yelling about you in the police station earlier. Trying to get the cops to charge you with harassing them."

"Okay, that means it's going to be far from easy."

"You got a plan?" she asked.

"Of course."

We drove another half mile before she spoke up again.

"What is it?"

"My plan?" I asked.

"Yes."

"Well, I was thinking of challenging George Hampton to a duel at sundown, pistols and all that."

"Uh huh. Something tells me they aren't going to go for that."

"Then I'm going with plan B."

"Which is?"

I hesitated, "I was contemplating asking them nicely to give themselves up. And if that doesn't work, I'll go to Plan C."

"Which is?"

"Working on that," I said.

CHAPTER FIFTY-ONE

THE NEXT MORNING, I WAS AT MY DESK, trying to get some paperwork from last month looked over and signed while at the same time trying to figure out how to take down George and Mary, when the door opened and Marcus Leon walked in.

I pushed myself the slightest bit away from my desk.

The guy caught even that miniscule movement.

"Relax, Quinton. I'm here under a white flag."

"Then I guess that means you're not armed or anything, right?"

The Hamptons' security chief grinned, though it looked a little strained around the edges. "Okay, let's say the flag is more dirty gray than white. Satisfied?"

"No, but I guess it'll do for now. What can I do for you? You come in here to go a few rounds?"

The guy snickered, kind of ego deflating considering how much smaller he was than me, and took one of my client chairs. I thought about coming around the desk and hauling him out of there to teach him some manners, then decided it'd be kind of undignified considering my gray hairs

Plus, I kind of worried he may be able to kick me around the room if he wanted to.

"No," he said after situating himself in my chair. "I don't want to take you on, Quinton. What I actually want to do is get out."

I shook my head, not sure I'd heard him right. "Excuse me?'

"I said I want out. I've had it with my employers."

"Why come to me?"

"Look." The guy leaned forward, clearly trying to project sincerity. "I'm not a nice guy, okay? I've done my fair share of smacking around in my time. The way I treated you when you first came to the house was only the first step. If I'd wanted to, things could have gotten really rough."

I smiled at him while flexing my right bicep. My tee-shirt sleeve swelled out about an inch or so.

"This kind of crap is too much," he continued.

Damn, the guy could have at least noticed the biceps.

"By crap, I assume you mean . . ."

"I'm a security man, Quinton. And a tough one if I have to be. I'm not going to sit here and say I've never killed anyone before, but I sure as hell don't go around randomly offing people. Or terrorizing old women in hotel corridors."

"Okay."

"And I sure as hell don't work for people who do or condone that kind of crap."

"And?" I said, just to keep myself in the conversation.

"You want the Hamptons, right? The keys to the kingdom? How about I give them to you?"

CHAPTER FIFTY-TWO

WE WAITED UNTIL FAIRLY WELL INTO THE NIGHT, the better to avoid complications. I eased the Cherokee up to the curb alongside the west side of the Hampton estate, right about where I'd been parked a few days before the first time I ran into Marcus.

After I shut the engine off, we sat there for a minute or two, each of us thinking our own thoughts.

"You sure about this?" I asked, breaking the silence.

Marcus shifted a bit in his seat, though he kept looking straight ahead. "I am. Like I told you, I've done my share of rough stuff in my life, but all of this is a bit too much."

"You didn't mind doing their work before," I pointed out. "What changed your mind?"

Marcus grinned, showing teeth almost too white. "Maybe I did a little test."

I looked sideways at him. "What sort of test?"

"Maybe I wanted to see just how deep they were into things before I decided how to proceed."

It took me only a second or two, and I felt like a simp for taking that long to put two and two together.

"You sent me the card. Pointed me in the direction of the right bank."

"You hang around these people long enough, you learn most of their secrets. They knew that Harris had something going with that bank, but not exactly what. As much as you'd been snooping around, I figured you'd know the what."

I thought it over for a while, drumming my fingers on the steering wheel.

"Doesn't add up," I said. "Exerting pressure to throw a trial is one thing. Murdering in cold blood is something else, though within the realm of possibility. But there's some stuff that doesn't make sense."

Marcus turned to look my way. "Such as?"

"Such as how did Sheila Hampton's prints get on the gun that killed Harris. If it's a frameup, that's stretching into the supernatural."

Marcus shook his head.

"I thought you were a detective," he said. "After everything you saw in that bank box, you can't figure it out?"

I stared out the window for a few minutes, my mind working it through. When it eventually clicked into place, the answer was so damned obvious I wanted to slap myself.

"They weren't her prints," I said.

Marcus shook his head. "Not even close. If those two old duffers in there can corrupt a judge or a prosecutor, you think some white bread who works in a crime lab is much of a challenge?"

I shook my head, almost not wanting to believe the enormity of the Hamptons' reach, not to mention their cruelty. "When they go down, there's going to be a whole lot of people feeling relieved."

"No doubt," Marcus said.

"May make it kind of rough for you to find a new job after this."

The security man grinned. "Don't worry about me, Quinton. I've worked for them for nearly eight years now. And every one of those years my salary's been in the low six figures."

"Sounds about right," I said.

The grin widened. "And the whole time I've been living as if I made thirty thousand or so. The rest has gone into ultra conservative mutual funds."

"In other words . . ."

"I have enough banked away to last me a good long time. Until long after George and Mary Hampton are forgotten."

I rolled my neck to work out a kink that had developed. "In that case, what are we waiting on?"

He laughed, faintly. "Damned if I know. You're the one shut the car off."

I grinned, then started the engine again. Following Marcus's instructions, I drove a ways, then angled my way into a side entrance to the estate.

Like the front entrance, this one had a small pillbox turret for a guard. Unlike my last visit, the turret was empty and the lights were dark.

"You sure the place is deserted?" I asked.

"I let all my guys go. Told them to work through ten tonight, then take off. Used my operating fund to give them hefty severance checks."

"That's awful close to embezzlement, isn't it?"

"It is. But if you bust this all open, a little thing like that is going to be the last thing for George and Mary to worry about."

I started the car forward again, then stopped before it had rolled more than five feet.

"Won't they be concerned when they can't raise any of their guards?" I asked.

Marcus shook his head. "Uh uh. Once they're in for the night, the place is like on autopilot. There are a couple of live-in servants, but even they actually stay in some of the guest cottages."

"You telling me that George and Mary spend their nights in that entire house by themselves?"

"That's what I'm telling you. Why?"

I didn't answer him at first, taking the time to work the thing out in my head.

"That means," I said a few seconds later, "they'd have plenty of time and opportunity to go out killing people."

Marcus turned to me, and even in the dim ambient light from the street behind us I could see his confusion.

"Wait a minute, man. I just assumed they were hiring people to do these killings and keeping me out of the loop. You trying to tell me you think it's those two old duffers themselves?" he asked.

I leaned forward over the steering wheel, trying to peer into the gloom of the estate.

"Could be," I said. "Both murders weren't exactly the neatest of things. And if they had some hired assassins coming in they've been doing it very quietly."

"Yeah, but. . ."

"Go back to the first one, Derek's murder. That was clearly an act of amateurs."

Marcus drummed his hands on his thighs for a couple of beats.

"I find it hard to believe those two old folks are that active," he said. "If you're right, we have to be extra careful going in there. And know this, it's George you've got to watch out for. They put on a good act, making it look like Mary is the sadist in the family. Actually, she's the follower. It's George who has the vicious streak."

Nodding in agreement, I took my foot off the brake and continued creeping into the Hampton estate.

THERE WERE A COUPLE OF SCATTERED YARD LIGHTS ON. Other than that the grounds were as dark as they'd looked from outside. I kept it to about three miles an hour, even though if someone were anywhere except the very front rooms they wouldn't hear a car approaching.

We pulled past the main front and angled toward a smaller side door about twenty feet to the right. At a nod from Marcus, I turned the ignition off and we exited the car.

"I'm guessing the doors will at least be locked," I said.

Marcus grinned. "Of course. Lucky for you the head of security's right here."

I grunted at that as we stepped up to the door. My companion reached into his pocket and pulled out a portable alarm pad and messed with the keys a bit. He glanced at me, and I reached out and opened the door.

"You have any way of telling if they're inside?" I whispered. As large as the house was, the whispering probably wasn't necessary, but I couldn't help myself.

It's not every day I break into the home of someone who can buy and sell me about a bajilion times over.

"Not with the portable," Marcus said back in a normal volume. "We'll just have to do it the old-fashioned way," he said.

I gave him the lead and we entered into the Hampton house.

Now if only the principals were home for the night.

CHAPTER FIFTY-THREE

THEY WERE.

My guts tightened a bit at how creepy of a scene it was.

We found them in one of the sitting rooms, Marcus had told me there were three, in the southwest corner of the house. Several minutes of catfooting through darkened hallways, past deserted dining rooms and kitchens, and around some of the most ornate furniture you could imagine, brought us within spitting distance of George and Mary Hampton.

If I'd been expecting some sort of epic confrontation, complete with threats, curses and maybe flying lead, I would have been disappointed.

Both of them were napping.

As Marcus and I stopped just outside the doorway into the room, we peeked in and saw both George and Mary, fully dressed except for being in their stocking feet, reclining in two easy chairs, one of brown leather and the other of some sort of green cloth, about ten feet from each other. I heard an almost inaudible snoring sound, and had to take a second look to confirm it was coming from Mary.

I glanced at Marcus, raised my eyebrows in question.

I also thought of what all my old fans would think if they could see the big, bad Blond Bomber hesitating on confronting a couple of senior citizens.

Seniors who had possibly killed at least three people that I knew of and blackmailed several others, but . . .

Shaking my head, I reached to the paddle holster at my rear hip and pulled out my gun. I noticed Marcus had his weapon out as well, some sort of sleek, black automatic that looked of foreign manufacture. Locking eyes, we silently mouthed 1, 2, 3, then moved in.

We were about eight feet away from them when Mary woke up.

She jerked upright, cutting herself off in mid snore, and her eyes fluttered as she struggled to make sense of what she saw. At first, a look of panic came into her eyes as she registered only two men who'd invaded her home. In a few seconds, she'd come enough awake to recognize us.

"Leon?" she croaked, her voice foggy with sleep. "What are you doing?"

Before either of us could answer, George mumbled a couple of times, swung his head back and forth, then sat up, awake and a bit more alert than I would have expected.

"Marcus?" Mary repeated, her eyes and face clearing as she came fully awake. "Was he trying to break in?"

"No, Mrs. Hampton. But we do have to talk to you."

"Talk?" Her eyes crossed in confusion. "George, what's he . .."

"It's over," I said.

The two of them glanced at each other, then back to us.

Mary sat up a little straighter, her eyes clearing as she came more awake. "Mr. Quinton, I don't know what you think you're up to, and it doesn't matter. Mr. Leon here will take care of you just as soon as . . ."

"No, Mary," Marcus said.

Now she turned her full attention to Marcus. "Excuse me?"

"I'm done working for you, and like the man said, it's over. I let him in here to get this settled, then I'm gone."

As the two of them talked, I glanced over at George. Where Mary looked slightly bewildered by the whole thing, George's complexion was turning faintly red, and I saw a steeliness in his eyes that I hadn't noticed before.

"I don't understand what you . . . ."Mary began, and I figured it was my time to jump in.

"Mike Palmer, Robert Harris, and your brother Derek. Tell me,

Mrs. Hampton, is that the extent of your crimes, or are there more? Oh, and let's not forget framing your sister in law for two murders."

Mary shook her head while George continued giving me that smoldering look.

"How's this your business?" she snapped at me. "How is any of this your business?"

"Maybe because I was hired to help get an innocent woman out of jail."

"Innocent?" George barked out. "The little slut was far from innocent."

"George," his sister cautioned, but the old man sat up straighter, his cheeks getting even redder.

"She was a little gold-digging whore from day one. Only dogging around Derek for the family fortune. Everybody in town could see it except for our simpleton brother."

I glanced over at Marcus, who looked about as confused as I was. Too much talk. I waited, wondering if they'd start demanding to call the police. Innocent people would have. Someone filled with righteous indignation, similar to what the two of them had shown earlier in Santiago's office, would have.

But these two were waiting it out, and that caused a little worm of anxiety in my gut. However, as long as I had them talking . . .

"What did you care about Derek's money?" I asked. "Or was it all a matter of family pride? You killed your brother just so he wouldn't embarrass the two of you?"

I'd made a shot in the dark, looking for some sort of rationale for all this insanity. And I got one, though not the one I'd expected.

"Hah!" George blurted. "Embarrass my ass. I don't know about sis here, but I wouldn't have given a damn about Derek's stupidity except . . ."

"George," Mary cut him off.

"Except what?" I asked.

"Forget it," George sneered. "I'm not telling you a damned thing."

"Maybe not," Marcus broke in, "but I'd like to know. If you didn't mind him marrying the girl, bringing someone so low class into your family, then what . . ."

"The money," I said.

"Huh?" Now it was Marcus's turn to look confused.

"Derek was the younger brother. Ordinarily, the family fortune would have been divvied up in more or less equal shares. Something tells me that didn't happen this time. Right?"

"Quiet, George," Mary said. "Don't tell him anything that could . . ."

"It's okay," George said. "Anything we say is just our word against his. But it would be kind of idiotic to give him any ammunition."

"Let me try then," I said. "I'm guessing that, maybe because he was younger, Derek was the preferred child."

"Hah!"

"And from what I understand your old man gave him control of the company, leaving you two out in the cold. Probably didn't make things better, did it? You two were probably left on the board, though, right?"

Almost total silence fell in the room. Almost, but not quite. Mary sucked in a little gasp of air while George's eyebrows knitted together.

I half turned to Marcus, though kept my eye on the two Hamptons.

"That was it, guy. Derek got control of the company and most of the funds when the old man passed away. These two were left out in the cold."

"No," Mary muttered.

"All that money in their kid brother's hands. Him and his trailer-park slut of a wife. Probably because the old man realized what a complete pair of screwups these two were and . . ."

Mary began fidgeting even more, causing me to keep more of an eye on her. The whole time, George had been sitting there fuming while his sister was starting to look manic.

In the next instant, I realized watching Mary had been a mistake.

"Gun!" Marcus yelled at the same time he jumped forward, knocking me out of the way and, though I didn't realize till later, himself as well.

I hit the floor and began rolling backward at the same moment I heard a booming roar practically in my ears. Marcus was lying half on me, and I felt him jump up then fall on me again before slowly sliding off.

I finished my backwards roll, at the same time pulling my weapon up and in line. Instinctively, since I'd had my eye on Mary up until everything went to hell, I swiveled my aim just a bit to the side and, sure enough, saw good old George on his feet, some kind of Godawful huge weapon bearing down on me.

Turned out later it was only a .38. Not that huge at all, but when your entire world is reduced to the vision of a gun barrel, it's going to look gigantic no matter the actual size.

I had time to get off only one shot before the instincts kicked in, making me roll again, to the side this time, just as George pulled his own trigger once more.

Somehow, his bullet managed to miss me, digging a furrow in the carpet only an inch from my face.

His bullet missed.

Mine didn't.

One of the richest men in the state, if not the entire U.S., flopped back in his chair, crimson staining the front of his shirt. As the reverberations of the two shots faded out, new sounds came to me.

Marcus Leon, to my side, gurgling and wheezing.

Mary Hampton somehow managing to shriek and gasp at the same time.

How was I going to explain all this?

Giving my head one last shake to clear the fuzzies out, I pulled out my cell phone and dialed Nichols's number.

CHAPTER FIFTY-FOUR

THE COPS SPENT MOST OF THE NIGHT going over the house and grounds. Although they had time for only the most cursory of searches, they managed to find more than enough to tag the two siblings for Robert Harris's murder, with the assumption that as they kept looking they'd find even more.

By the time I left, somewhere around three, I'd been grilled up one side and down the other by a frowning Lt. Santiago before I was allowed to go on my way, the usual "don't leave town" speech ringing in my ears.

Sheila Hampton was formally and completely released from the care of the state at eight thirty the next morning. Later, one editorial on a local newscast noted that it was a marker of how monumentally the state had screwed up that the court system had opened half an hour earlier than usual to accelerate her release.

The proceeding itself, no doubt all ironed out beforehand in the judge's chambers, took no more than fifteen minutes. And it ended with the delicious irony, straight out of a movie script, that as Sheila was walking out of the courthouse, wearing blue jeans, a Banana Republic tee-shirt and sandals instead of a county jail jumpsuit, and with her hair freshly done, Mary Hampton was ushered in one room down to face another judge for her initial arraignment.

Neither George nor Marcus had made it through the night.

The two parties didn't exactly pass each other halfway down the hall. That would have been too much to hope for even if everyone in the building knew exactly what was transpiring.

I was on hand to witness the proceedings, even though I had no actual need to be there. After a quick handshake from Sheila before she went to meet with the press and a couple of quick words with Bernie, I headed out of the courthouse, climbed into my Cherokee, and drove home to sleep the sleep of the dead.

The next morning, rested, refreshed and with a three-egg omelet, a rasher of bacon and three cups of coffee from my favorite breakfast café resting in my belly, I headed into The Blaster.

Knowing I was going to be around, Lisa had taken the day off to run some errands, and around eleven that morning Keri Eckland and I were in the midst of cleaning and buffing the Nautilus machines when I looked up to see Karyn Roberts walking in the door.

I finished scrubbing the particular machine arm I was working on before capping the cleanser bottle and standing up. By that time, Karyn had made her way over to me.

Keri looked up from where she was sitting down polishing, must have caught the vibe right away, and stood up, heading over to do some trivial paperwork behind the counter.

Karyn parked herself on the bench of a machine next to the one I was working on.

"How you doing?" she asked.

I gave her a manly shrug and put the polishing rag down. "Better than I was this time yesterday," I said.

"There going to be any legal ramifications on your end?"

"Bernie called last night, and he said not to worry. I have to go in later this afternoon to give an official statement, the hours Santiago spent grilling me don't count, and we'll have to go before a pro forma hearing in a week or so, but everyone pretty much agrees I'm in the clear. And if I'm not, I think I know someone who works for a good legal defense group."

Karyn smiled. "If it's the group I'm thinking of, they only come into play after someone's been convicted."

"Oh, darn," I said.

Her smile sobered up a bit. "You entered their home illegally."

"Technically, I was invited in by their head of security, but I see your point. The problem is, there's so many people in the political structure around here running for cover that I don't think they're going to worry much about me."

"Well, if nothing else, you got Sheila off the hook."

"Yeah, and I'm sure she's eternally grateful."

"Have you heard from her?"

I stood up and dropped the polishing rag. "Nope. As of last night neither has Bernie. Once they left court yesterday morning she took off."

"She's a very confused woman right about now," Karyn said.

"She's also in line to be a very rich woman once everything gets untangled. You guys going to help her with that?"

Karyn shook her head. "Not in our purview, though we can give her some names of reputable financial people to help her out."

The front door opened, and a couple of middle-aged women, regulars, came in and headed back to the locker rooms.

Karyn stood up.

"Heading home?" I asked.

She said, "Time to get back to the regular job, at least to keep the office from falling in on itself."

"You could hang around for a few days. If you ask me, you've earned a couple of days off."

"Maybe," she answered. "Though I doubt my daytime clients would think so."

I wondered where the old magic had gone

"Swing back around first chance you get," I said, "and I'll take you out for some more authentic BBQ."

She grinned, her green eyes crinkling.

"Or you could come out my way, and see what the real thing actually tastes like."

"I guess I could at that."

She held out her hand. "Take care, Mr. Quinton."

"Blondie," I said, making sure I didn't crush her hand in my grip. "My friends call me Blondie."

A high-school teacher, former college instructor and fiction writer, Kevin R. Doyle is the author of three crime thrillers, *The Group*, *When You Have to Go There*, and *And the Devil Walks Away*, published by MuseItUp Publications, and one horror novel, *The Litter*, published by Night to Dawn Magazine and Books. Last year saw the release of the first book in his Sam Quinton mystery series, *Squatter's Rights*, by Camel Press. Doyle teaches English and speech at a high school in central Missouri.

www.kevindoylefiction.com